Shisir Basumatari is an artist who works with body painting and photography. He has exhibited his work at the Delhi Photo Festival in 2011 and was the art director of the short film *Seven Hundred Zero Zero Seven*, starring the Assamese writer Ranju Hazarika, which went on to win the Golden Conch for best documentary at the Mumbai International Film Festival in 2014.

He likes to cycle, and is currently restoring an old 1985 car. Interestingly, his father was a zoology lecturer and people often praised his beautiful handwriting. It is no coincidence then that he ended up working on a project involving terrible handwriting.

DISCLAIMER

Shisir Basumatary really exists.
He did find my father although he still can't read Baba's handwriting.
He is good at other things as well – badminton, stage-sets, and growing beans.
He is not very comfortable reading Assamese.
I could not get him to stop after a few years.
He has since returned most of my father's diaries.
He has very little to show for the last ten years of his life, neither did my father at his age.
But now this is done, what a big relief it is.
I can hear my father chuckling with glee at the thought that his bad handwriting has been good for something after all.
Besides reading all sorts of unusual stuff, he is also a film buff.
Like my father, he likes keeping to himself.
This book was originally conceived of as a book (with text), then as a film (with animation), before it became an 'animated' book.
Hope all of this fits into one page.
I hope he doesn't turn out like my father.
There have been times I have been very cross with him.
When he began with this project he was still quite young.
I am worried that my father will not let go of him.
Is this my father's biography? One always needs something to write about.
A creative masterpiece – thank you for letting me be part of it.
Not just that, actually, thank you Shisir.

Meenaxi Barkotoki

THE REAL MR. BARKOTOKI

Shisir Basumatari

TIGER PRINT

SPEAKING TIGER BOOKS LLP
125 A, Shahpur Jat, Near Asiad Village
New Delhi 110049

First published by Speaking Tiger 2019

The publication of this book is supported by the Munin Barkotoki Memorial Trust

ISBN: 978-93-89231-65-6

10 9 8 7 6 5 4 3

To the people of Dudhnoi,
for giving me the space to explore.

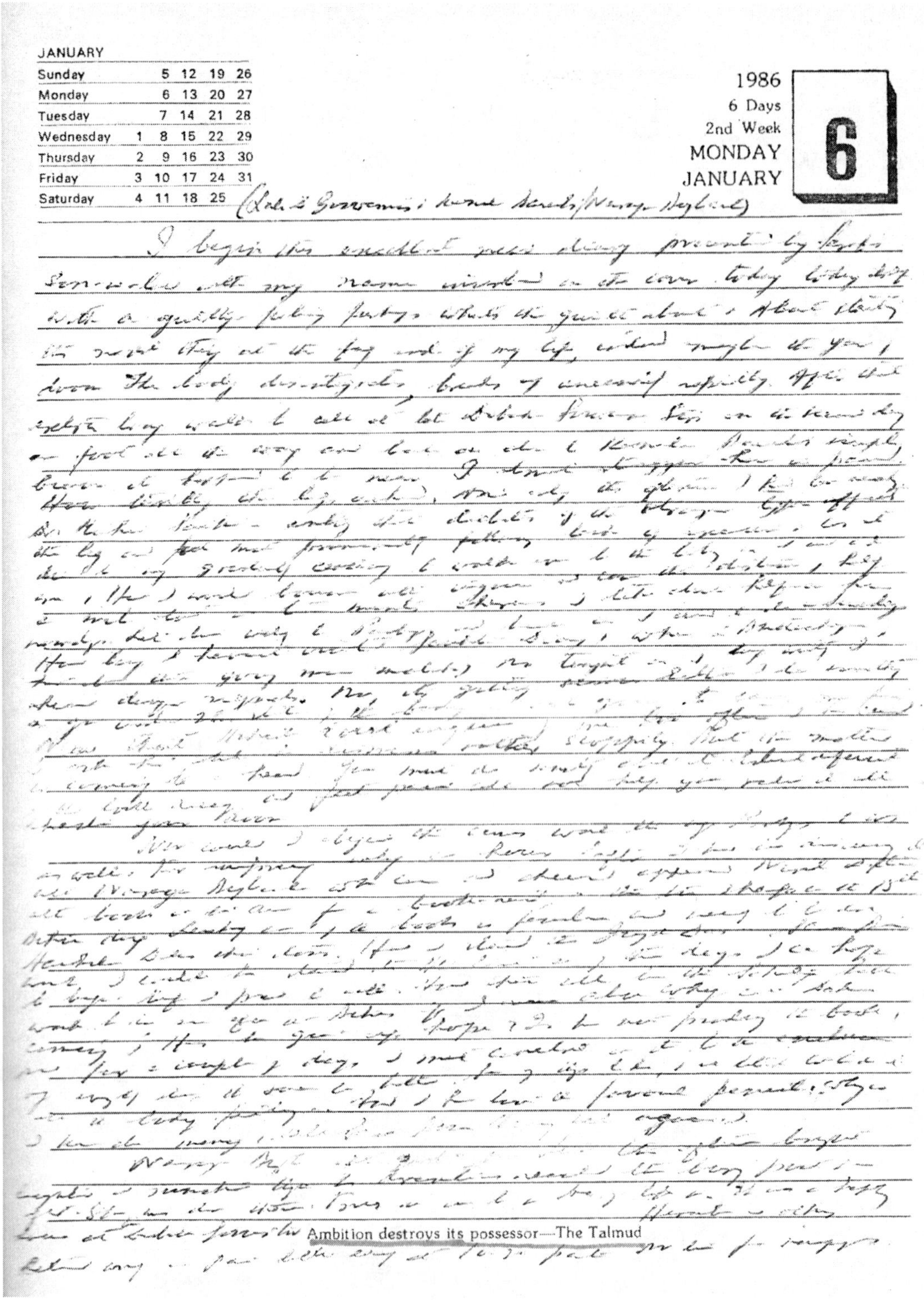

JANUARY

Sunday		5	12	19	26
Monday		6	13	20	27
Tuesday		7	14	21	28
Wednesday	1	8	15	22	29
Thursday	2	9	16	23	30
Friday	3	10	17	24	31
Saturday	4	11	18	25	

1986
6 Days
2nd Week
MONDAY
JANUARY
6

Ambition destroys its possessor—The Talmud

A page from the diary of Munin Barkotoki

PROLOGUE
Our sitting began on a dramatic note. Doctor Das delivered his opening lines... "We spend roughly twenty years asleep. Dreams are important."
tik tik tik tik tik tik tik
But it's not my thing to LET IN.
"Do we have our patient-doctor confidentiality?"
Doctor Das nodded.

You might think... A Doctor? No. I'm not sick. I see a dream... I see myself walking into a house... What is this house? The problem is, I SEE IT EVERY NIGHT
But, if I am going to tell everything to the doctor... I'd better deal with this discomfort first— the discomfort of letting someone read your diaries, or that of an author writing her autobiography. They are the same...

FOUR WORDS
First Draft needs a lot of editing & correction
MY FATHER AS I KNEW HIM
Meenaxi Bhattacharjee
'To thine own self be true
And it shall follow, as the night the day.'
This was the one single belief that guided and shaped Baba's life. If he had a motto at all, it was his abiding faith in the truth and validity of the above lines from Shakespeare.
It is very hard to write about my father in the past tense. For he still lives — in my thoughts and memories and those of others, as well as in his own written and recorded words. He also lives on, in me. It is even harder to attempt to make a list, even if incomplete, of what I owe my father. I owe the very gift of life to him. Not only that, while my mother tried to teach me how to survive, my father helped me to understand why one needs to survive at all.[1]

He was a full half century older than me
As such I do not know Baba in his youth
or middle age.
Even in my earliest recollections of him
he is tall, handsome, dignified and
an imposing figure, past his prime,
impeccably dressed in a spotless white
dhoti and a stiffly ironed kurta.
The most enduring image of my father
however, was of him sitting quietly in
his room, reading, or listening to the
transistor.[2]
Dr Meenaxi Bhatt

Mister Barkotoki, when you were in J.B. College, Krishna Kanta Handique was the Principal. How did his presence influence you?

AT THAT TIME, IT WAS KNOWN AS JORHAT COLLEGE. WE WERE THE THIRD BATCH. I DID NOT HAVE ANY PERSONAL RAPPORT WITH K.K. HANDIQUE. He usually came in the evening. Only occasionally he used to conduct our English literature periods. SO IT IS HARD to tell if there was any direct influence.

Although surprisingly even without knowing him in person, he seemed/to have left a tangential mark on me.

As a person, a scholar, his wisdom left a thirst for knowledge in me.

He was well-known then as a pandit, a researcher, and a polyglot.

He must have left an indelible impression on me; Else I wouldn't have revered him all my life.

After our marriage it looked like Barkotoki was more keen on reading than writing.
He was around 45 when we married.
Barkotoki never sent his writings for publishing. Whenever I asked, he'd say, "I've to go through them once."
HE WAS NEVER SATISFIED WITH HIS OWN WRITINGS
Even as a journalist, he'd often have differences with the establishment or the editor and he'd quit his job.
Letters to the editor and the critical essays, he wrote them with regularity and used to send them. But since no one could read his handwriting, he often had to use his typewriter.
Renuka Devi

हवाई पत्र
Aerogramme

Ms. Meenaxi Bhattachariya (Poupee)
112 SUMMERTOWN HOUSE
369 BANBURY ROAD
OXFORD UK
OX2 7RD

Panchaboti, GAU   17 June, 92

Poupee dear,

I wonder whether it will be a surprise or a shock for you to have got a typed letter from me this time. When last did such a thing happen in the long last three years if ever?

It was great relief and delight to receive your aerogramme after your long silence on the 15th just a week after you had written. You had legitimately complained my handwriting was getting even worse than before putting you to much trouble in reading it toterably comfortably. Immediately I recalled how late Kokaideo, your Bardeuta, have had to make the same complaint years & years back in the forties advising me to write a bigger hand or stop writing. What a pity my handwriting could'nt improve even in half a century. Since there was no possibility of any change at this stage of life this time I have, interestingly, struck upon this typing idea rather providentially, if that's the right word. I shall keenly wait to know how you react... In a better state of mind & body. Not only me. Amlan Baba too was at his cheery best when I told him how his mumu anxiously waited for a letter from him ....

18 June Thursday

Could you imagine from a place like Oxon (?) what could happen at such a half-way house point on Wednesday afternoon to compel me leave off? Electricity snapped when it was only 6pm not to return until after 8pm night and toda[y] I am in no mood to continue wha[t] with a heavy head & severe bout of depression, seized me.

(2)

Poupee dear, I have started writing a Thursday evening. [illegible] ... should I have taken days to complete a letter. Attempting typing [illegible] another mistake [illegible] good mood the [illegible] typewriter was not [illegible] for years. [illegible] I would [illegible] writing to you. But doing that [illegible] ... afternoon [illegible] to concentrate [illegible] for the [illegible] of [illegible] here. [illegible] and [illegible] have [illegible]

To return to [illegible] of things I would [illegible] I had have no [illegible] dear Bar [illegible] happens [illegible] to [illegible] company of [illegible] my [illegible] self of any worry–

1 THE REAL Mr. Barkotoki

RK
DANCE
SCHOOL
MUNIN
BARKOTOKI
GUWAHATI

Wake up!

SLEEP
WELL

A MUNIN BARKOTOKI
MISCELLANY

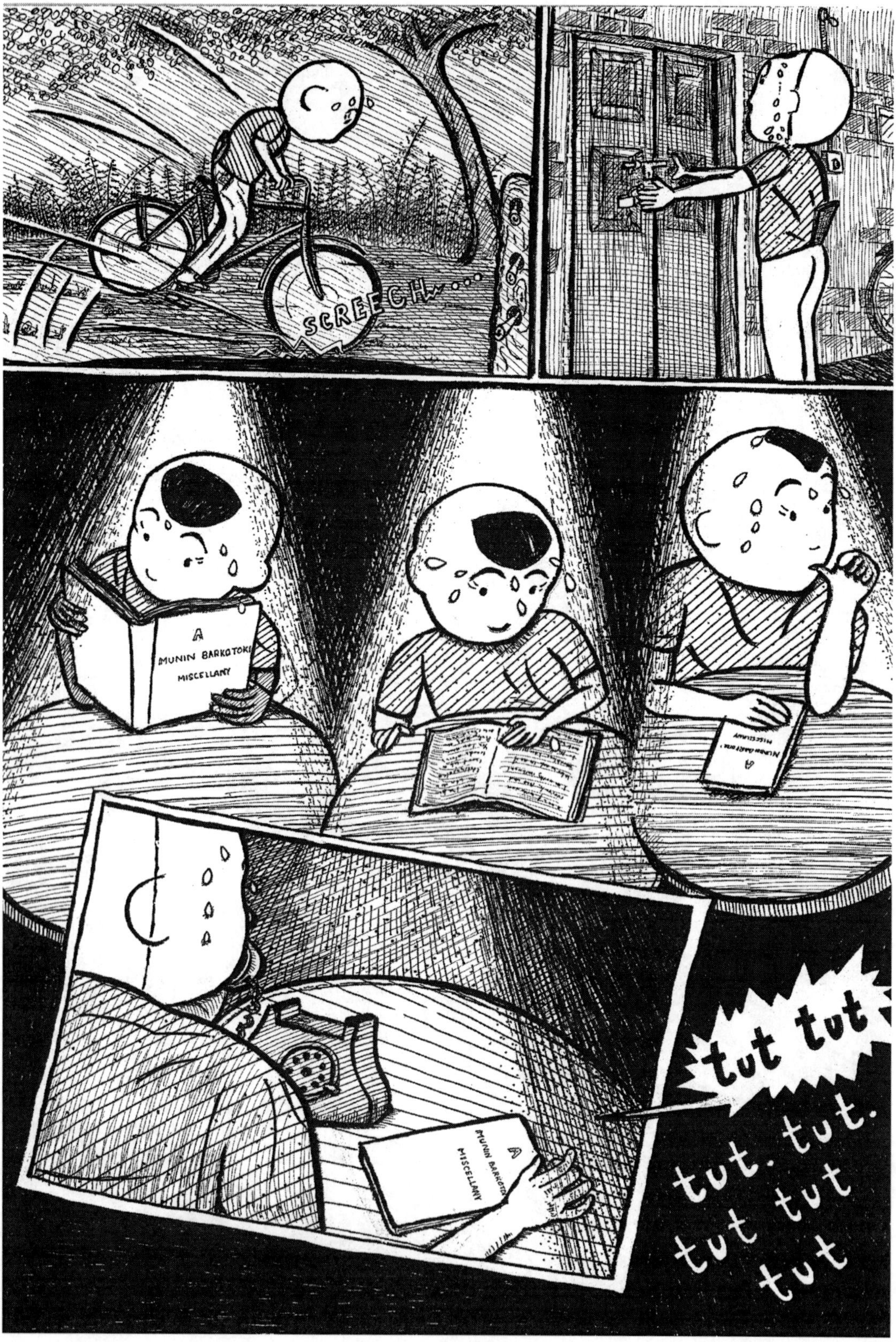

SCREECH...
A
MUNIN BARKOTOKI
MISCELLANY
tut tut
tut. tut.
tut tut
tut

No Signal
TRING
CAPTAIN D speaking.
Book!
What Book?
Kidding me?
MUNIN BARKOTOKI!

AFTERWARD...
CAPTAIN D
KLINK!
I think I am losing it.
And the book? Did you read it?
I don't know.
I think. Yes I did.
Sanity... insanity. You, me, the people on the street... None can tell one from the other.

You mentioned a doctor on the phone.
FIRSTLY where did you find this?
In fact, why not recount it from the start.
A MISCELLANY
MUNN DARKOTONI
Recount what? It's just bits and pieces. You heard them.
TALKING HELPS. Here pour some.
A MISCELLANY
MUNN DARKOTONI
ANOTHER!
ANOTHER!
THUD!

It was a year ago...
When it first came.
Made little sense.
A refill? And it's alright.
Dreams don't make much sense anyhow.
I would've let it pass.
Only that it keeps coming.
The same dream...
night after night
MUNIN
BARKOTOKI

Dew on winter's grass
Marching under hazy sun
Revealed here one plan
Only remember
Barkotoki is a God fearing man

COME...I was waiting for you
Barkotoki is a GOD-fearing man...
Barkotoki is a GOD-fearing man...
So you can't let it go?
Here is a complete book on Munin Barkotoki! Come on

5
Foreword
A distinguished mind of our
times, Munin Borkotoki (1915-93)
was a man of wide-ranging
curiosity and exceptionally varied
interests. His passions included
literature, journalism, theatre,
film, music, painting, sports and
of course - politics. Though his
literary output was sparse —
consisting almost wholly of just
twelve stories and sketches, five
poems or pastiches, a one-act
sundry essays, notes, belles-
letters to the editor and a
biographical studies (Bismrit
TWO THINGS...
ONE. MUNIN BARKOTOKI EXISTED FOR REAL.
TWO. HE IS DEAD.

2 SHELL SHOCKED

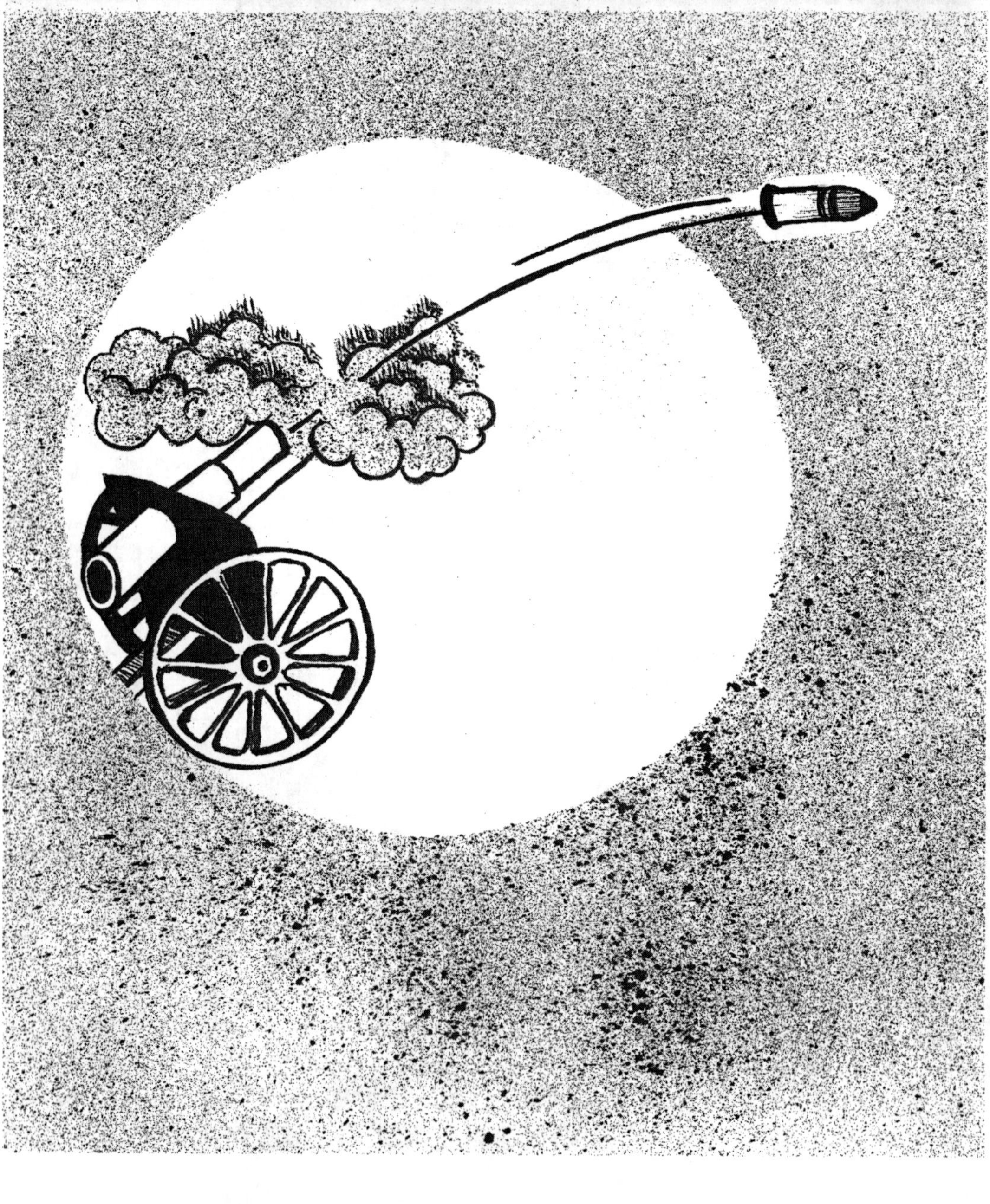

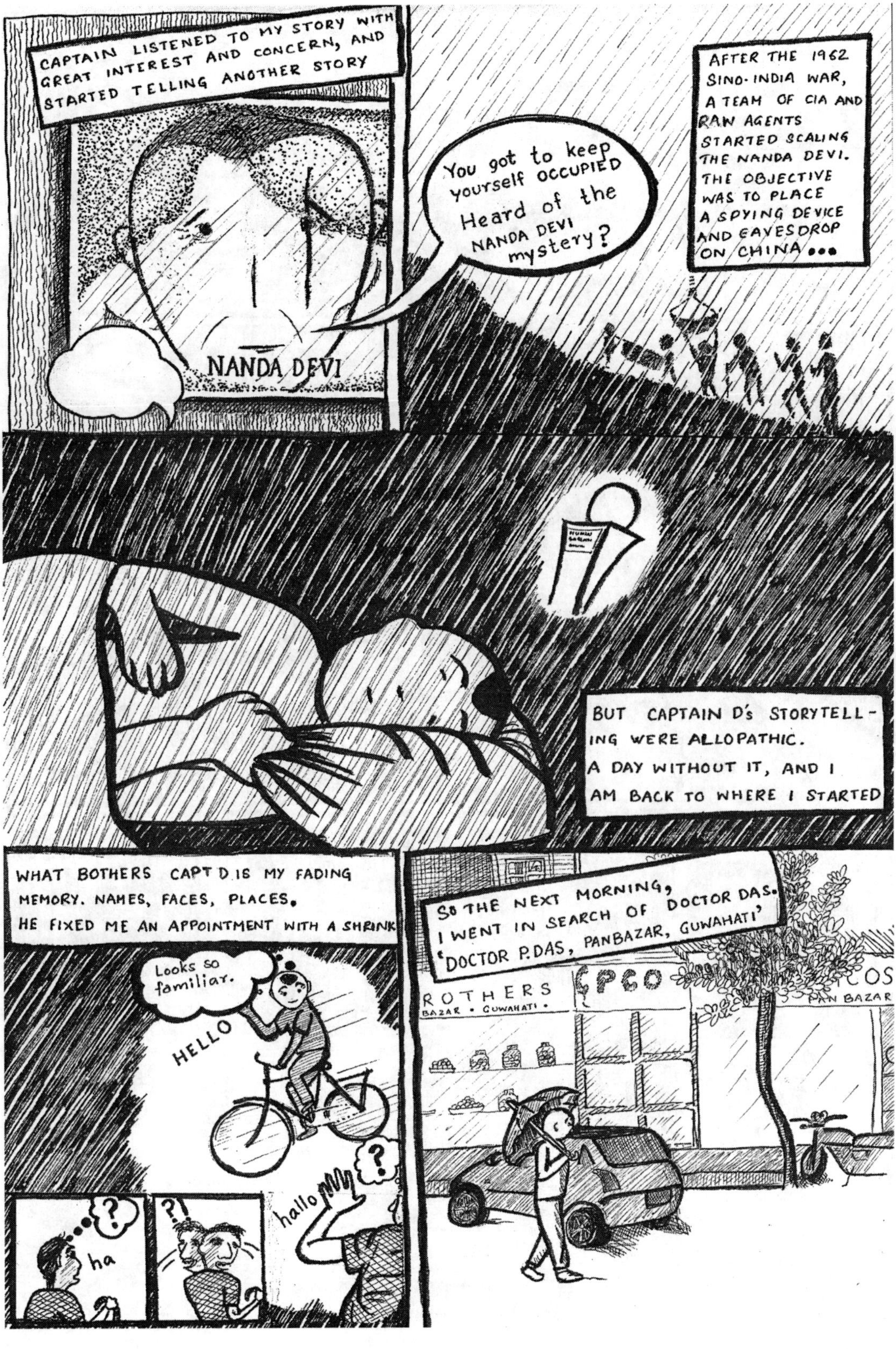
CAPTAIN LISTENED TO MY STORY WITH GREAT INTEREST AND CONCERN, AND STARTED TELLING ANOTHER STORY
NANDA DEVI
You got to keep yourself OCCUPIED
Heard of the NANDA DEVI mystery?
AFTER THE 1962 SINO-INDIA WAR, A TEAM OF CIA AND RAW AGENTS STARTED SCALING THE NANDA DEVI. THE OBJECTIVE WAS TO PLACE A SPYING DEVICE AND EAVESDROP ON CHINA...
BUT CAPTAIN D's STORYTELL-ING WERE ALLOPATHIC. A DAY WITHOUT IT, AND I AM BACK TO WHERE I STARTED
WHAT BOTHERS CAPT D IS MY FADING MEMORY. NAMES, FACES, PLACES. HE FIXED ME AN APPOINTMENT WITH A SHRINK
Looks so familiar.
HELLO
?
?
ha
?!
hallo
SO THE NEXT MORNING, I WENT IN SEARCH OF DOCTOR DAS. 'DOCTOR P. DAS, PANBAZAR, GUWAHATI'
ROTHERS
BAZAR • GUWAHATI •
CPGO
COS
PAN BAZAR

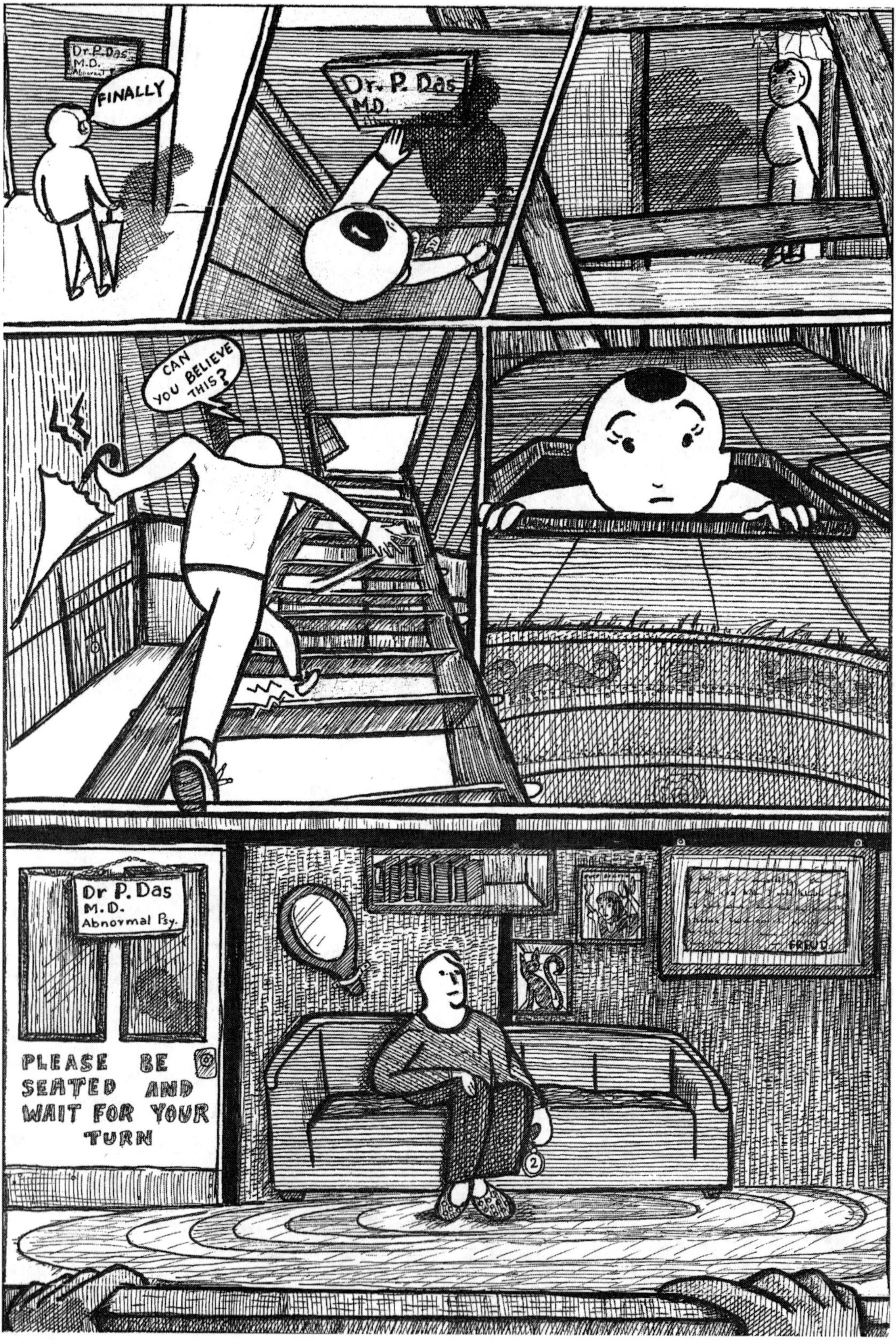
Dr. P. Das
M.D.
FINALLY
Dr. P. Das
M.D.
CAN YOU BELIEVE THIS?
Dr P. Das
M.D.
Abnormal Psy.
PLEASE BE SEATED AND WAIT FOR YOUR TURN
FREUD
2

Doctor P. Das? I had an appointment
TIC TOC TIC TOC TIC TOC TIC TOC
Yes Sir Please take your token and have a seat.
PLEASE BE SEATED AND WAIT FOR YOUR TURN
"It still strikes me myself as strange that the case histories I write should read like short stories and that, as one might say, they lack the serious stamp of science. I must console myself with the reflection that the nature of the subject is evidently responsible for this, rather than any preference of my own." FREUD
TIC TOC TIC TOC TIC TIC TOC TOC
SOON...
Oh! I love this place. Um except the stairway
I almost had a heart attack on those stairs. Just kidding. It's my first day here.
SORRY TO INTERRUPT, SIR. NO 2 CAN NOW GO INSIDE
TIC TOC TIC TOC

hope we meet again
CLICK
Sure!
TIC TOC TIC TOC
TIC TOC TIC TOC
TIC TOC TIC TOC
SIR YOU MAY GO IN NOW
?
CLICK
COME IN PLEASE
YOU?
YES HAVE A SEAT

SORRY ABOUT THAT LITTLE CHIT CHAT OUTSIDE PROCEDURAL... YOU KNOW
ANOTHER TRICK?
WHAT'S THIS?
THAT'S YOUR FILE
Case no: 3295
SHELL SHOCK MEMORY CLINIC GUWAHATI
FROM CAPTAIN D. HE PICKED A FORM FROM HERE A WEEK AGO
FILLED IT UP FOR YOU. AAH, MOSTLY BLANK.
WE GOT TO FILL THEM UP TODAY.
• IS HE REAL?
• I DON'T THINK SO
OKAY. SO IT SAYS
YOU CANNOT SLEEP
YOU SEE A DREAM
AND HE BELIEVES, YOUR MEMORY IS HEADING SOUTH
AND Based on our little chit chat, outside, I'll add. SOCIALLY AWKWARD
CAPTAIN D
•TEA LOOKS REAL
•SMELL IT
Doctor. Before we go about filling those BLANKS... Where do we Stand?
DEPENDS!
On how you look at it. The way I see it, we sleep for roughly 20 years. Dreams are IMPORTANT
NOW Let's get to WORK

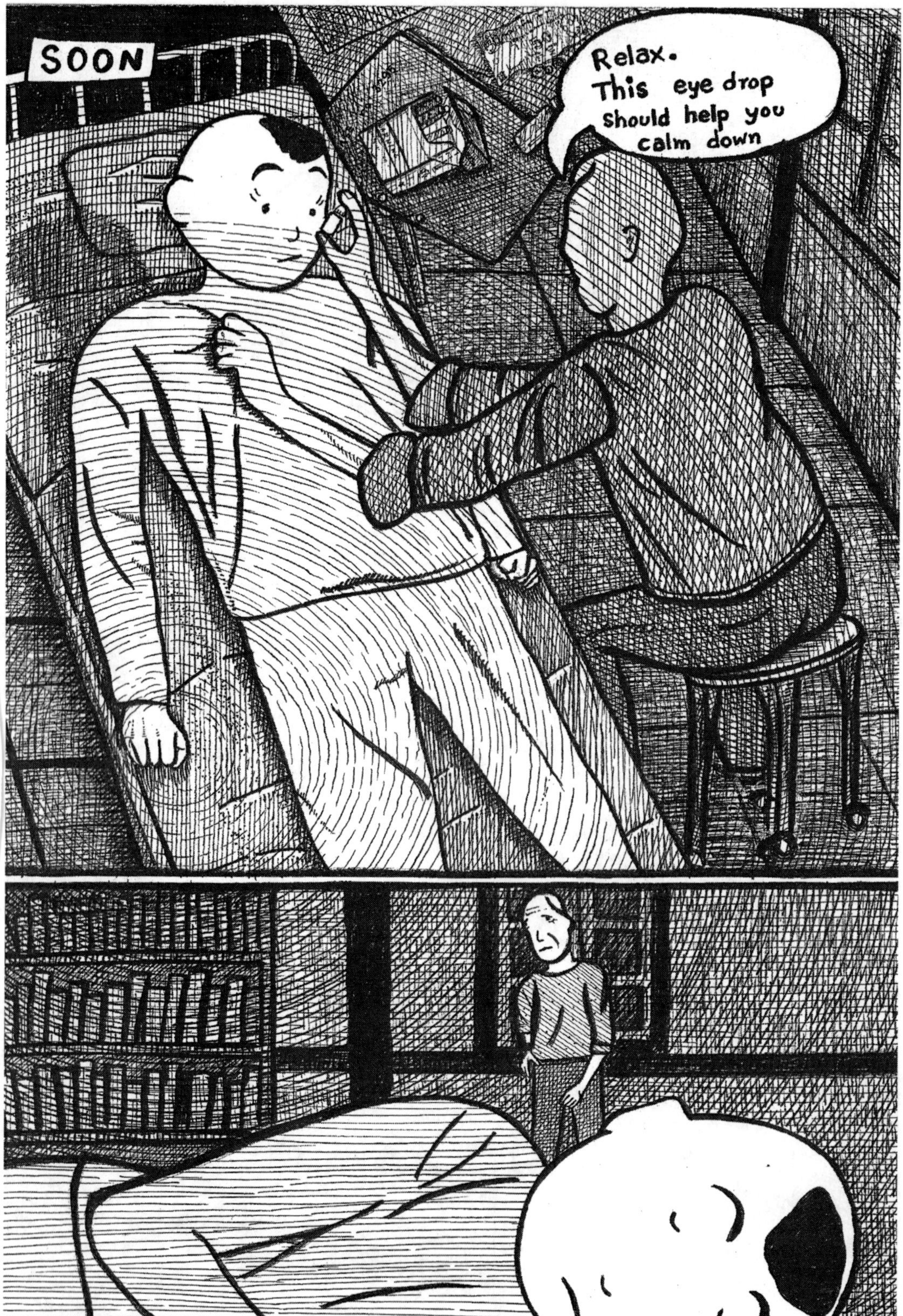
SOON
Relax. This eye drop should help you calm down

SHELL SHOCK
CLINIC
BOOK STATION
BAZAR. GUWAHATI
How did it go?
Something else please... Nanda Devi?
Sure. Where were we?
1965. So two dozen sherpas and several CIA and RAW agents started climbing for the NANDA DEVI summit. The sherpas carried food supplies and other regular equipments. They also had to carry the SECRET device and a PLUTONIUM powered generator, nicknamed GURU RINPOCHE by them.
The sherpas were unusually enthusiastic about carrying the generator. Do you know why?
It was because of the heat that the PLUTONIUM was generating.

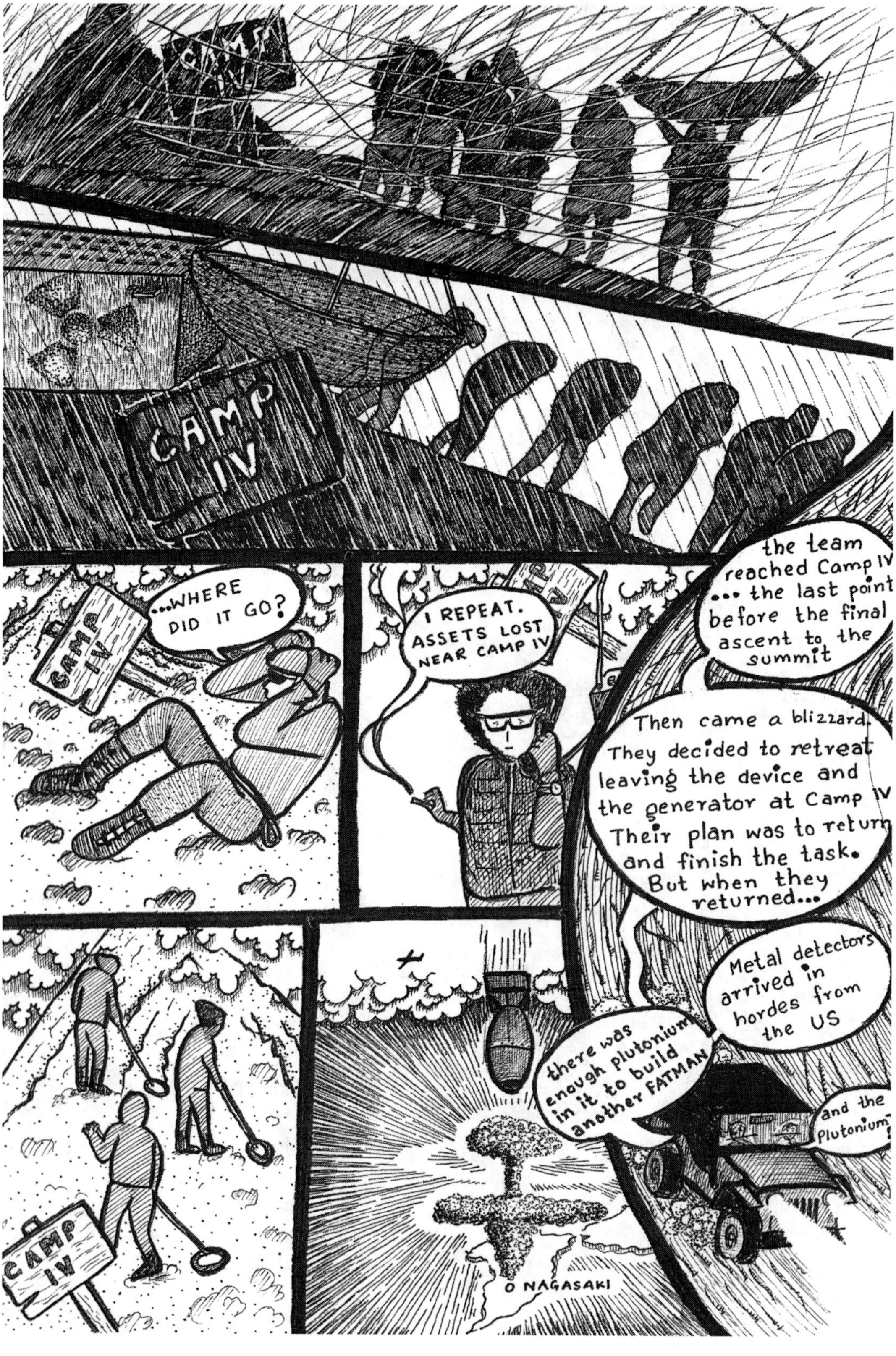
CAMP
CAMP IV
CAMP IV
...WHERE DID IT GO?
I REPEAT. ASSETS LOST NEAR CAMP IV
the team reached Camp IV ... the last point before the final ascent to the summit
Then came a blizzard. They decided to retreat leaving the device and the generator at Camp IV Their plan was to return and finish the task. But when they returned...
Metal detectors arrived in hordes from the US
there was enough plutonium in it to build another FATMAN
and the Plutonium!
CAMP IV
O NAGASAKI

(*)

In 1968, around the same time when Nanda Devi swallowed the plutonium, a 'gamma irradiator' was imported for use in Delhi University. It was discarded in 1985 and after years of lying on the lawn, scrap dealers dismantled it in Delhi's Mayapuri scrapyard... The cobalt in it killed and affected the people involved.

MUNIN BARK
A MUNIN BARKOTOKI MISCELLANY
I began to read the book. It had the names of a few people who knew the late Munin Barkotoki.

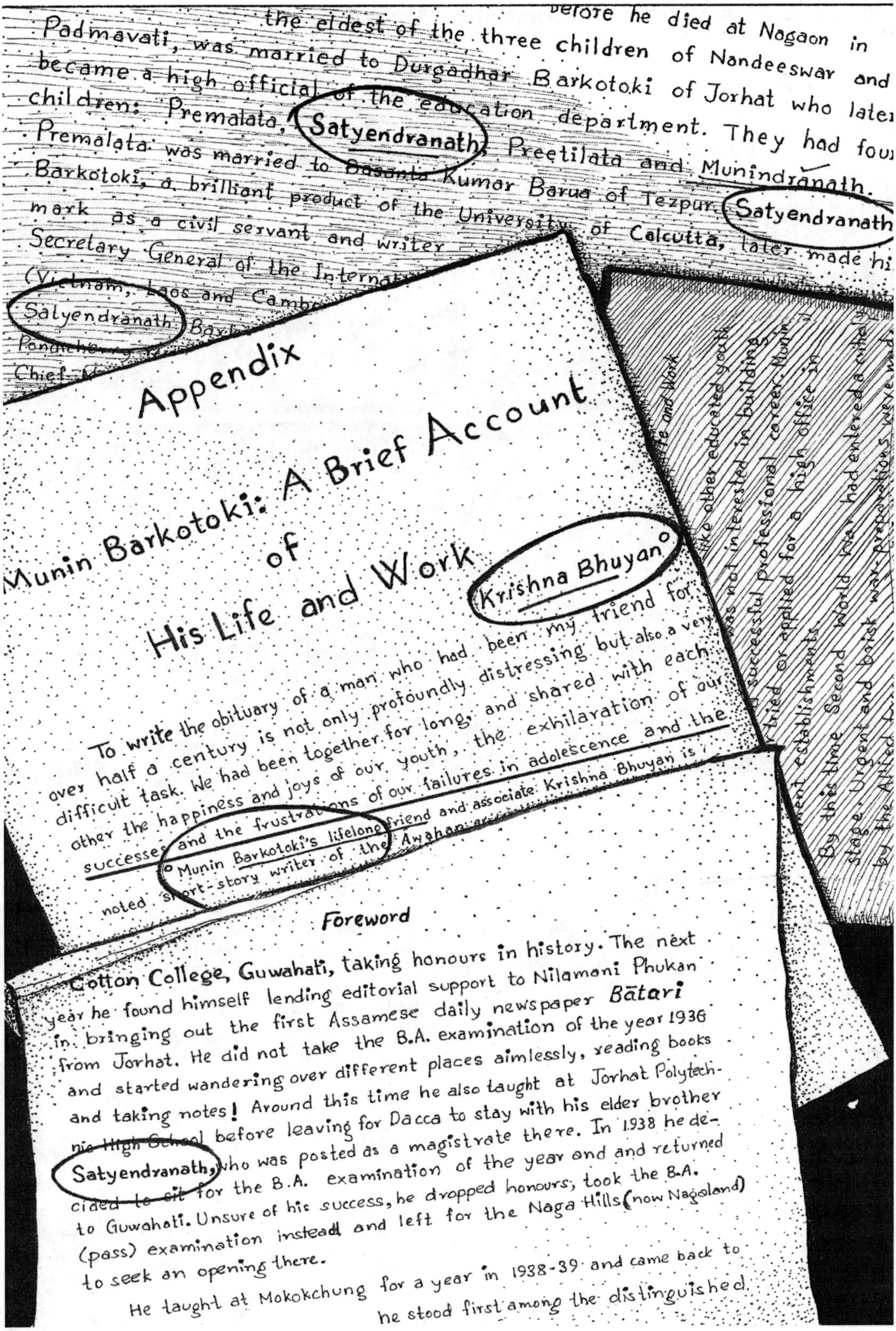
before he died at Nagaon in
the eldest of the three children of Nandeeswar and
Padmavati, was married to Durgadhar Barkotoki of Jorhat who later
became a high official of the education department. They had four
children: Premalata, Satyendranath, Preetilata and Munindranath.
Premalata was married to Basanta Kumar Barua of Tezpur. Satyendranath
Barkotoki, a brilliant product of the University of Calcutta, later made his
mark as a civil servant and writer
Secretary General of the Internat
(Vietnam, Laos and Cambo
Satyendranath Bark
Pondicherry
Chief
Appendix
Munin Barkotoki: A Brief Account of His Life and Work
Krishna Bhuyan°
To write the obituary of a man who had been my friend for over half a century is not only profoundly distressing but also a very difficult task. We had been together for long, and shared with each other the happiness and joys of our youth, the exhilaration of our successes and the frustrations of our failures in adolescence and the
° Munin Barkotoki's lifelong friend and associate Krishna Bhuyan is a noted short-story writer of the Awahan era.
Foreword
Cotton College, Guwahati, taking honours in history. The next year he found himself lending editorial support to Nilamani Phukan in bringing out the first Assamese daily newspaper Bātari from Jorhat. He did not take the B.A. examination of the year 1936 and started wandering over different places aimlessly, reading books and taking notes! Around this time he also taught at Jorhat Polytechnic High School before leaving for Dacca to stay with his elder brother Satyendranath, who was posted as a magistrate there. In 1938 he decided to sit for the B.A. examination of the year end and returned to Guwahati. Unsure of his success, he dropped honours, took the B.A. (pass) examination instead and left for the Naga Hills (now Nagaland) to seek an opening there.
He taught at Mokokchung for a year in 1938-39 and came back to
he stood first among the distinguished
Life and Work
like other educated youth
was not interested in building
successful professional career. Munin
tried or applied for a high office in
establishments
By this time Second World War had entered a critical
stage. Urgent and brisk war preparations were made
by the Allied

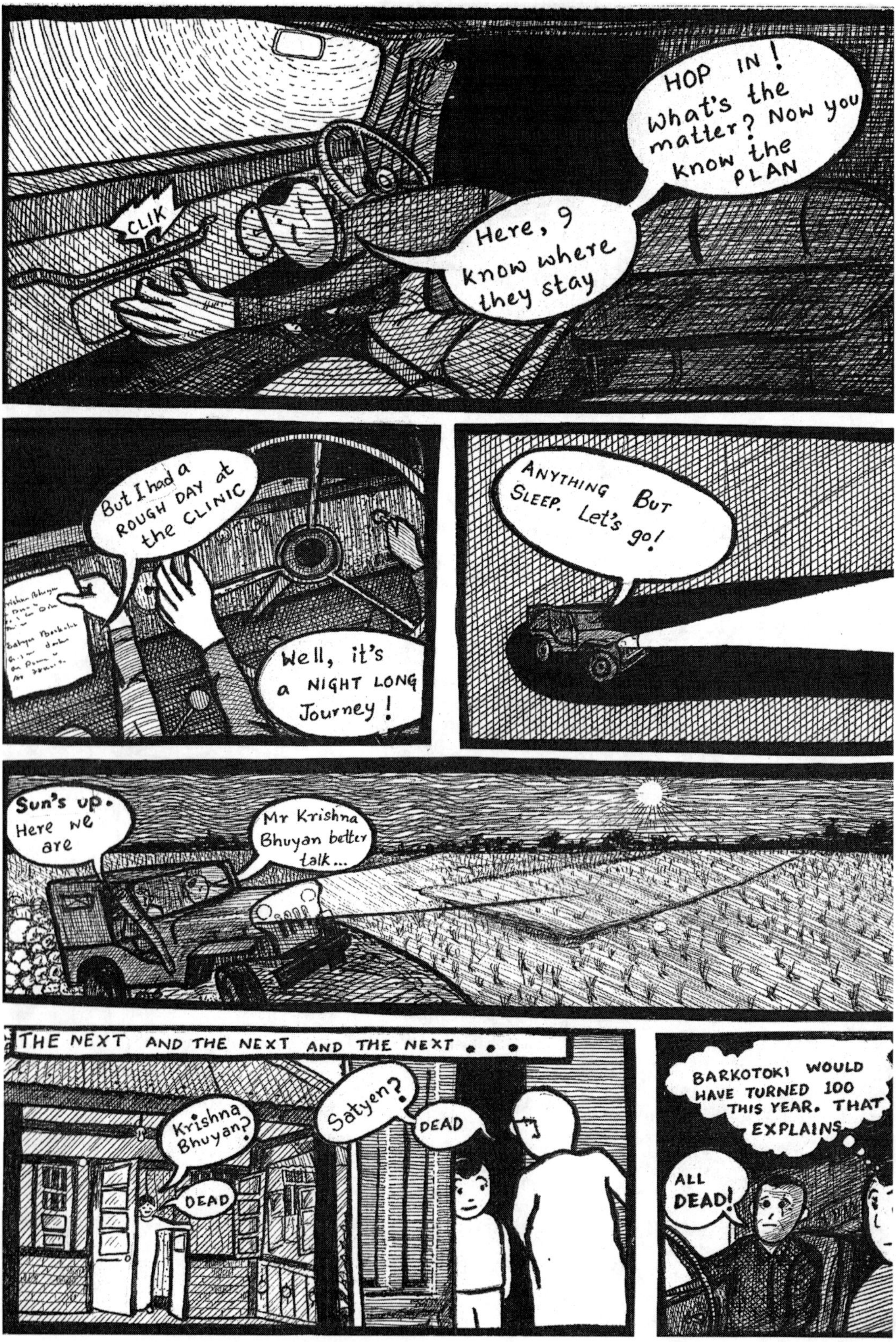

CLIK
HOP IN! What's the matter? Now you know the PLAN
Here, I know where they stay
But I had a ROUGH DAY at the CLINIC
Well, it's a NIGHT LONG Journey!
ANYTHING BUT SLEEP. Let's go!
Sun's up. Here we are
Mr Krishna Bhuyan better talk...
THE NEXT AND THE NEXT AND THE NEXT . . .
Krishna Bhuyan?
DEAD
Satyen?
DEAD
BARKOTOKI WOULD HAVE TURNED 100 THIS YEAR. THAT EXPLAINS
ALL DEAD!

We still have a plan. PLAN B
Last night
THIS fell out of the BOOK
It's yours now
MUNIN BARKOTOKI AWARD CEREMONY
2 MARCH, 2013, SATURDAY
EVENING 4
VENUE: VIVEKANANDA AUDITORIUM
UZAN BAZAR, GUWAHATI - 1
MUNIN BARKOTOKI MEMORIAL TRUST
SILPUKHURI, GUWAHATI - 3
ASSAM
He had to rush. Engine oil leaking
Eh. Still. Bit of a coincidence,
Of all the days...
it had to be the 2nd of March
2013
SATURDAY
VIVEKANANDA KENDRA
MUNIN BARKOTOKI AWARD CEREMONY
2 MARCH, 2013, SATURDAY
EVENING 4
VENUE: VIVEKANANDA AUDITORIUM
UZAN BAZAR

3 Dr. Baruah's SPEECH

Now I invite to the stage
the recipient of the 2012 Munin
Barkotoki Award
Shri Sarmistha Pritam
Now I am reading out
the citation letter
MUNIN BARKOTOKI AWARD PRESENTATION
Dear Sarmistha Pritam, we are very happy to have your autobiography 'a personal chat' as the recipient of the 2012 Munin Barkotoki Award. Heartiest congratulations...
...By writing an autobiography at such a young age you have set a new milestone in Assamese literature.[7]

now I request Dr Dilip Baruah
to deliver his speech
on the 'yardsticks of criticism'
zzz
wake up!
TODAY MORNING CALAMITY STRUCK
THE FOUNDER OF THE TRUST
SHRI RENUKA DEVI FELL ILL
WE WERE CONCERNED IF OUR MEETING WOULD TAKE PLACE
I WAS INVITED TO GIVE A SPEECH, LEAVING IT ON ME
TO DECIDE THE SUBJECT MATTER
MY OLD FRIEND ARUN SARMA TELEPHONED ME AND ASKED
"CAN YOU COME?"
I SAID NO AS I HAD OTHER WORK
BUT ON SECOND THOUGHTS I LATER REALIZED I STILL HAD A WEEK
I DECIDED TO GO
MUNIN BARKOTOKI AWARD PRESENTATION
2 MARCH, 2013, SATURDAY, 4 PM
VENUE: VIVEKANANDA AUDITORIUM
UZAN BAZAR GUWAHATI-1
I have been writing a piece on the yardsticks of criticism. When I asked Meenaxi, if it will be of any use, she sounded very eager and said, "IF BABA WERE ALIVE, HE WOULD HAVE LOVED TO HEAR THIS."
She put me in trouble by saying that and raising her expectation to that extent... that I'm feeling a bit ILL AT EASE. 'CRITICISM' does not fit in an occasion like this, amidst festivity because often times it involves shedding blood. IN REALITY I'M FEELING TOTALLY OUT OF SORTS.

During the 1940s we always heard the names Krishna Bhuyan
and that of Munin Barkotoki taken together.
Munin Barkotoki's name is remembered distinctly as a man,
of rare intelligence and passion for knowledge.
Although the late Munin Barkotoki and I hail from
the same area in Jorhat... on one side of the river
Bhogdoi was his family and on the other was ours...
I did not have any notable acquaintance with him,
Until I went to Shillong for my newly appointed
job at the Anthonys. I checked into the Sanatorium.
At that time Barkotoki was also staying there.
One day I walked up to him and introduced myself
He appeared to be brooding during those days
His close friend Krishna Bhuyan once said
that Munin Barkotoki's marriage with a lady
like Renuka Devi was a positive thing that
changed the course of his life.
And I'm speechless to see their daughter Meenaxi's
dedication towards the Munin Barkotoki
memorial trust and in knitting a small
fabric of the young Assamese
intelligentsia.
UNBELIEVABLE!
a complete
speech on criticism
in my memory
Sir
Yes
THERE'S a saying, A SON IS A SON
TILL HE GETS A WIFE
BUT A DAUGHTER IS
A DAUGHTER
ALL HER LIFE
Many feel that the afterlife of a writer is more
important than his...?

ONCE AGAIN, THANK YOU ALL FOR BEING HERE TODAY.
ONE IMPORTANT ANNOUNCEMENT. THERE ARE BOOKS FOR SALE...
BOOKS
LATE MUNIN BARK
SIR, STEP IN PLEASE. ALL BOOKS AT 50% DISCOUNT!
Highlights:
• A Collection of his hand written letters.
• A Collection of his letters to the Editor
• AND Much more!
SPECIAL DISCOUNT
BREAK GLASS

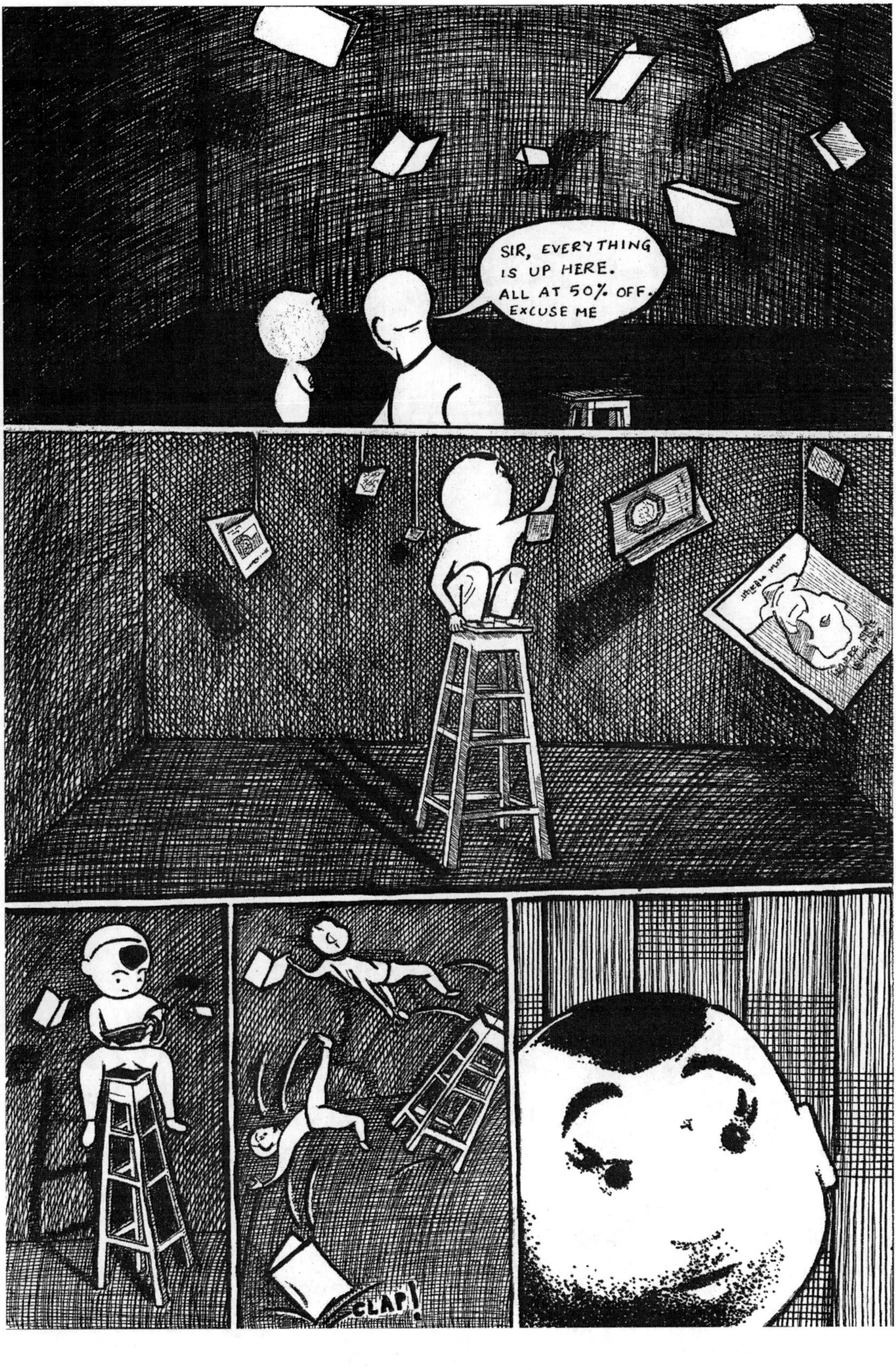
SIR, EVERYTHING IS UP HERE. ALL AT 50% OFF. EXCUSE ME
CLAP!

clap
CLAP
CLAP
clap
CLAP
THAT WOULD BE 350. NO SIR. WE'VE GIVEN 50% OFF ALREADY!
YES MA'M 50% off. But, only for today

MUNIN
MISCELLANY

VIVEKANANDA

4 BARKOTOKI DIARIES

So here's everything on the late Barkotoki
THE KEY TO YOUR DREAM

TWO DAYS LATER
A MUNIN BARKOTOKI MISCELLANY
MUNIN BARKOTOKI
Huh! Think I found something
as Bhuyan Jetha* has hinted in his article, he did not believe in achieving immortality by creating something of lasting value. He saw little reason to exert himself over things which could have little significance in the overwhelming magnitudes of the vastness of our universe. In that vast scale, it simply did not matter whether he wrote or didn't.
Another less profound reason suggests itself. Baba had an atrocious handwriting, barely legible even to Baba himself. Small wonder then that many of the articles and letters he wrote were never published. He wrote a diary daily almost all his life, and there are many such diaries which need to be read. Maybe they contain a lot of valuable information about his mind and life. One cannot say unless one has 'deciphered' them first. But that job seems extremely difficult and we have found no takers yet.
There was
more tangible reason for his being
so erratic a
writing — his poor health. Baba
was
ailment or the other since the late
adies continued, in one form or the
end. His physical problems were further
mental shock he got in the early eighties
বিভিন্নজনৰ দৃষ্টিত মুনীন বৰকটকী
১৪৮

These Barkotoki diaries. We need them. Here's my plan... ... ...
but the solution sounds crazier than the problem Capt D
crazier? I'll tell you what's crazier. It's going to bed with that dream every night.
MUNIN BARKOTOKI SILPUKHURI GUWAHATI
Anyhow what are you complaining about? You just drive!

THUD!
Let's go!

That's the mask maker's home. Stop by that tree
WHAT? Have you seen a ghost? I need to look younger!
and MUTE. That's important
EXCELLENT! Drop me at the Barkotoki house now. I'm getting us the DIARIES.

Alright!
YOU CAN TAKE YOUR ID BACK
These are my father's diaries
WAIT for a moment
It's unfortunate that you can't speak. This 'Lettera' belonged to my father. Can you type your thoughts on these diaries? Briefly
Lettera
TIC TIC TIC
HARIJAN
AHMEDABAD
Continued from page 02
your diary must contain every particular about your health. It must also contain the particulars of work done every hour, if the work could be so divided. You might also make it a mirror of your own mind, recording your thoughts and dreams, good and bad. This mirror of the self is helpful for a purification of one's self.
Madam,
In an article in "বিশিষ্টজনৰ দৃষ্টিত মুনীন বৰকটকী," you mentioned your father's diaries.
You also mention his illegible handwriting and his reverence for Gandhiji.
By the way, Gandhiji was a diarist; he used to read his diaries in public speeches and he exhorted his fellow satyagrahis to maintain diaries.
Madam I think this is a mutually beneficial pact. With access to these diaries, I get to further my research; you get to know what's...
Did she get you the DIARIES?
YES! Hurry let's g
AXA 3295

**

Who is Wolfman? Wolfman aka Sergei Pankejeff was Freud's most famous patient. In fact he is the most famous patient in the field of psychoanalysis. Pankejeff sought Freud's intervention in order to overcome a dream that he had seen as a very young child.

A couple of years after his treatment with Freud, Pankejeff developed a psychotic delusion and was seen walking on the streets staring at his reflection on a mirror.

5 THE HABIT

Dr P. Das
MD
Abnormal Psy.
TIC TOC
TIC TOC
SWOOSH...
TIC
TIC
TOC
REM NOTED. OVER.
TIC TOC SWOOSH...
TOC
SUBJECT AWAKENING. OVER.
TIC
TOC
SWOOSH...
subject awakening
over.
TIC TOC TIC TOC
Swoosh...
can you hear me?
FICTION
TIC
TOC
TIC
TOC
"It still strikes me myself as strange that the case histories I write should read like short stories and that, as one might say, they lack the serious stamp of science. I must console myself with the reflection that the nature of the subject is evidently responsible for this, rather than any preference of my own." FREUD

Can you hear me?
Yes Doctor
Your form now looks complete. But I have two quick queries.
Case No. 3295
Here are your personal belongings, a pen, some money etcetera.
This cassette makes me wonder about the music that you must be carrying with you.
But, before that can you explain the diaries, that you mentioned
A

OH
YES
That night...
After we reached Capt D's house, with the diaries, he went off to read them straightaway
I sat to watch T.V.
THE EXORCISM RITUAL RESULTS IN A SPECIFIC BRAIN ACTIVITY THAT CUTS THE PERSON OFF FROM THE POSSESSION EXPERIENCE. BUT EMILY'S EXORCISM COULD NOT HAVE ACHIEVED THIS... BECAUSE THE DOCTOR GAVE HER GAMBUTROL
After a while Capt D re-appeared looking for Something
Thanks. I got it.
Can I help you?
WHAT DO YOU BELIEVE WAS THE RESULT OF TREATMENT WITH THIS INTOXICATING DRUG?
GAMBUTROL LOCKED EMILY IN THE POSSESSED STATE

Dr. P. Das
MD
Abnormal Psy.
I returned home the next day, leaving Capt D with the diaries of Barkotoki
KURT VONNEGUT
God Bless You, Dr. Kevorkian
Wake up!
SLEEP WELL
and went off to sleep

WHAT DO YOU SEE?
NOTHING
KURT VONNEGUT
God Bless You, Dr. Kevorkian

★"Many years ago in Guwahati, we had the opportunity to watch an individual walking on a specific road every evening. At a certain time he starts from his home at Panchabati and reaches the District library. After spending

Some time there, he would walk back to his home. Watching him in this manner everyday, I was reminded of Kant. Kant's outings were so routine that people could set the time looking at him."

– Barman, Sibnath. "*Munin Barkotoki: a rare individual.*" Proxakh, August, 1982.

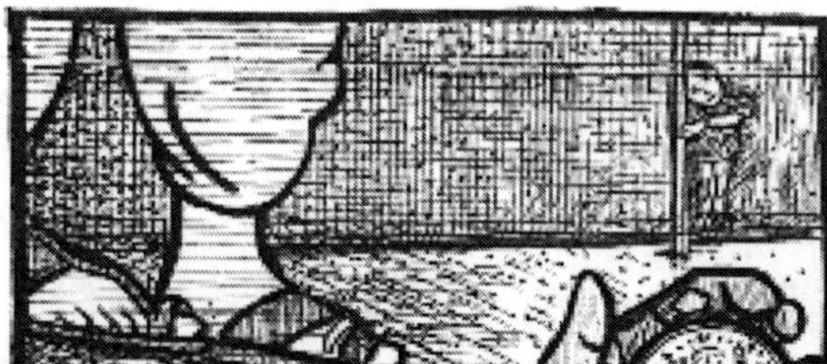

...at some time, normally in the evening I used to walk to the library. At times I'd stay there for longer, sometimes shorter. Went there primarily to read international papers that cannot be had at home, reference books and sometimes I'd simply go when I found it difficult to find an answer to something while at HOME. Add to it, there was always something or the other happening in the auditorium. I MUST ADMIT THIS HAD TURNED INTO A HABIT*...
* HABIT 'An Eye witness' account by KUMUD GOSWAMI
"One day Barkotoki sir spotted me on the footpaths of Silpukhuri
DISTRICT LIBRARY
Are you writing anything?
Thankfully we reached the library before I could answer
Soon, Sir immersed himself in his study. I hovered around aimlessly, before settling under the dysfunctional clock, beside the library caretaker.
He won't leave. Not until I shut the doors and the windows. EVERYDAY! Does he read so much?
Couldn't tell if the person was angry or surprised. So everyday, Sir would walk to the library and return in the evening. THAT WAS ONE HABIT."

wheeer
PLAY
FF
PAUSE
CLICK
Shri Barkotoki, you are a well-known writer in Assam. There were other well-known writers known to you. Who were they? And how did they shape your writing?
STOP
As writers, we were known as writers from the 'AWAHAN' প্ৰজন্ম — generation. Amongst all the writers, Krishna Bhuyan was my closest. HE IS STILL ALIVE. Famous short story writer. There were others like Laxminath P
CLICK
TIC TOC TIC TOC TIC TOC
swoosh REM NOTED over.
FREUD
TIC TOC TIC swoosh
subject in deep sleep state. over... TIC TOC

TIC TOC
TIC TOC
SWOOSH

DO YOU SEE YOURSELF?
I'm driving

I'm stopping now.
I have something. Some newspapers.
IEW

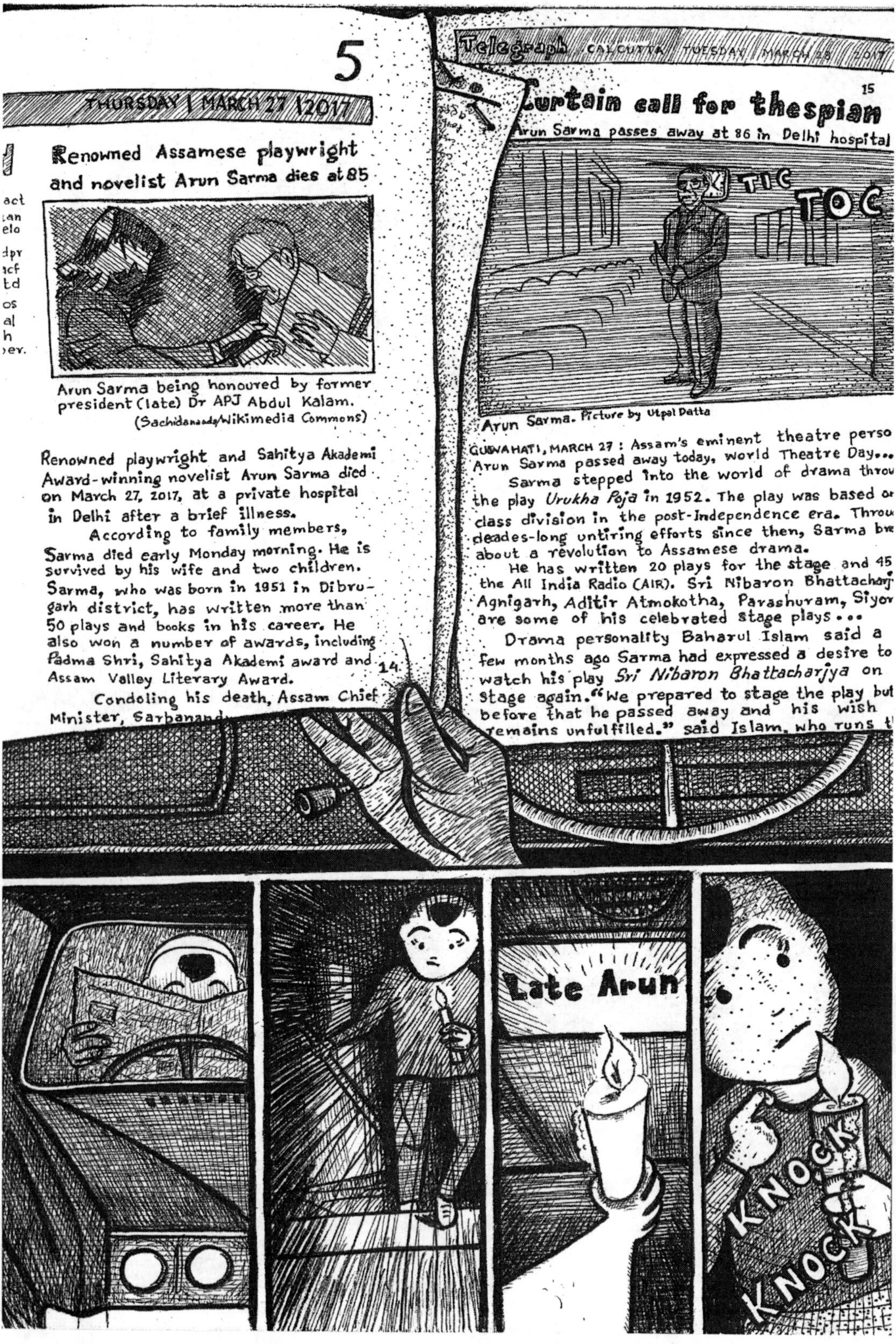
5
THURSDAY | MARCH 27 | 2017
Renowned Assamese playwright and novelist Arun Sarma dies at 85
Arun Sarma being honoured by former president (late) Dr APJ Abdul Kalam.
(Sachidananda/Wikimedia Commons)
Renowned playwright and Sahitya Akademi Award-winning novelist Arun Sarma died on March 27, 2017, at a private hospital in Delhi after a brief illness.
According to family members, Sarma died early Monday morning. He is survived by his wife and two children. Sarma, who was born in 1951 in Dibrugarh district, has written more than 50 plays and books in his career. He also won a number of awards, including Padma Shri, Sahitya Akademi award and Assam Valley Literary Award.
Condoling his death, Assam Chief Minister, Sarbanand
14
Telegraph CALCUTTA TUESDAY MARCH 28 2017
15
Curtain call for thespian
Arun Sarma passes away at 86 in Delhi hospital
TIC
TOC
Arun Sarma. Picture by Utpal Datta
GUWAHATI, MARCH 27 : Assam's eminent theatre perso
Arun Sarma passed away today, world Theatre Day...
Sarma stepped into the world of drama throu
the play Urukha Poja in 1952. The play was based o
class division in the post-Independence era. Throu
decades-long untiring efforts since then, Sarma br
about a revolution to Assamese drama.
He has written 20 plays for the stage and 45
the All India Radio (AIR). Sri Nibaron Bhattachar
Agnigarh, Aditir Atmokotha, Parashuram, Siyor
are some of his celebrated stage plays...
Drama personality Baharul Islam said a few months ago Sarma had expressed a desire to watch his play Sri Nibaron Bhattacharjya on stage again. "We prepared to stage the play but before that he passed away and his wish remains unfulfilled." said Islam, who runs t
Late Arun
KNOCK
KNOCK

WHO BARKOTOKI?
Put out the fire. stay quiet
hate Arun
CLICK
WHO ARE YOU? I WANT TO TALK ABOUT BARKOTOKI... ARE YOU ARUN SARMA?
MUNIN BARKOTOKI
rma
I will.
Ssh!
Sssh
Why, Papa, do you go on shouting? There's not a soul in front of you. No, Papa, noone has come to see our play.
Ishall present to you today. And on hearing it... you will know, you will realize, what sacrifices one has to make, what miseries, misfortunes and odds one has to fight to create something great, to evolve a novel art. Yes, I too have had these fights and cheerfully have I lost and won...
Nibaran Bhattacharya by Arun Sarma

CLAP
CLAP
CLAP
CLAP
Sir, where can I find Arun Sarma
You are speaking to him
Sir how did you know Munin Barkotoki?
Everyone knew Munin Barkotoki
I rememb-er reading his stories in Awahan when I was in school. Let's say late 1940's
AWAHAN
GANDHIJI
SUPPRESSION BLUES
1940's... AWAHAN ... short stories... when did you meet him?
1960's... District Library auditorium. He used to be a regular – to our shows. He would walk to the Library, read, attend shows and walk back. In the 1960s Assamese drama was passing through an important period and Barkotoki... he had a role to play.[16]

Sir, can you elaborate a bit on Barkotoki?
Munin Barkotoki died in 1993. Few years later, I'd written an article for a book on him.
'Munin Barkotoki's love of theatre'
Arun Sarma
TIC
TIC
TIC
You see, towards the late 1940s, a trend surfaced in Assamese theatre. Established writers shying away from writing plays. Barring a few like Jyoti Prasad Agarwalla and Atul Chandra Hazarika, most had abandoned plays as a form of literature.
भारत
INDIA
500 ज्योतिप्रसाद आगरवाला
JYOTIPRASAD AGARWALLA
Why? Was there a REASON?
Primarily, the rapidly evolving light and sound technology. Writers all of a sudden, were required to familiarize themselves with the stage. Many, found it tough and couldn't accept this as routine.
Yet the theatre groups needed plays to stage. Directors, actors and theatre lovers started writing plays. Assamese theatre, stripped off of its literary value, turned towards spectacle.
This further alienated the writers and the intelligentsia. Soon there wasn't any one left to speak or write on Assamese theatre
UNGODLY INTERVIEW WITH
LATE ARUN SARMA
. MB's love of theatre
But Barkotoki?

By 1952, I'd started writing plays for the radio. I was teaching in the village then.
Who is it from?
Munin Barkotoki
It was a postcard written by Munin Barkotoki in his small running scribble.
Munin Barkotoki was a regular listener of 'RADIO THEATRE' aired by Akaxbani, Guwahati. He wrote the postcard after he listened to one of my plays on the radio.
THIS IS ALL INDIA RADIO AND...
Did you meet Barkotoki?
Not until 1960. That's when I'd come to Guwahati to join the job at Akaxbani.
From then on he was my most important critic and my inspiration in writing plays. From 1960 until his death, he was a routine patron to all the shows at the District Library auditorium and at the adjacent Rabindra Bhawan. In the absence of an invite, he'd even pay the gate fee to a show. Such admiration towards Assamese theatre, by a literati was indeed very rare, during that time. Barkotoki wasn't the kind of audience, who having drawn his entertainment, goes home and forgets all about it. After watching a play, as he would silently walk on the footpath, leading to his home in Panchabati, Barkotoki would carefully weigh the play from all angles.
What is this play Nibāran Bhaṭṭacārya about and where is its kernel?

Interesting... Now what can I tell you about Baba. This typewriter for instance...

*'Lettera' also means dirt in Assamese.

TIC TIC TIC TIC
can you tell me about his daily routine, or his habits?
My father was half a century older than me. Even in my earliest recollections of him he was past his prime.
There's one thing In the early 70s on most evenings, he'd walk the straight road to the District Library.
As that road was so familiar, he seemed to walk almost in a reverie. Baba had this strange habit of Sometimes writing even while walking. One such evening, I saw my father walking towards home...
What is this drama *Nibāran Bhaṭṭacārya* and where is its kernel? Satyaprasad Barua, who is one of the more knowledgeable amongst us about things theatrical, sums it up as being the portrayal of a conflict between a talented and experienced playwright and his unresponsive, unsympathetic philistine society and avers that the drama suffers from poetic excess...[17]

...he was wearing the routine spotless white dhoti and a stiffly ironed khadi kurta.
But there was a problem ya. There was a manhole, gaping open. My father, unaware of it, was busily writing and walking towards it.
!
while Nibāran Bhaṭṭacārya is evidently about that kind of conflict it is also definitely something more, and the other charge of POETIC EXCESS does not to my mind detract from its dramatic quality. Arun Sarma's Nibāran Bhaṭṭacārya reminds me of what the powerful film-maker Godard once said about another all-time great in the other medium, Ingmar Bergman: "ONE IS ALWAYS ALONE ON THE STAGE AND BEFORE THE UNWRITTEN PAGE. AND TO BE ALONE FOR BERGMAN MEANS TO ASK QUESTIONS." That too is of the essence in regard to Nibāran Bhaṭṭacārya with the difference that the playwright Nibaran Bhattacharya finds himself alone in the auditorium and the
artistic world for that matter, not at the beginning of his spiritual Odyssey but at the end of it when the society for whose entertainment and enlightenment he had staked his all, had no use for his creative labours and punished him with an EMPTY HOUSE.
Nibaran Bhattacharya's tragedy is the tragedy of an intense artist, a poet if you will, cheated of his life's dream at the climactic moment of his career and made to stare at a society without a soul. How can such a life be be dramatized except by resorting to near-frenzied flights of poetic fancy? Far from being charged with failure to keep within the constraints of drama, Sarma should..
...get all the kudos in the world for being able to impart such potency and intensity to a drama of incident as distinct from a poetic drama or drama of the Eugene O'Neil or Strindberg kind.

He did not even recognise me for a few seconds and stared at me, wondering what business a strange girl could have to come and fling herself on him...
He later told us that he had actually managed to perform that descent several times before. Given his tendency for dream-walking, I wasn't too surprised.
ha
ha
ha
Poupee you just saved me from descending into the underworld of GMC*. Thank You!
* Guwahati Municipal Corporation

Damn mosquitoes! What's taking him so long
MUNIN BARKOTOKI
Oh, here he comes
MUNIN BARKOTOKI
GUWAHATI
Got em?
Yes HURRY Let's go.

IN BARKOTOKI
LPUKHURI
UWAHATI

6 REAL BAD HANDWRITING

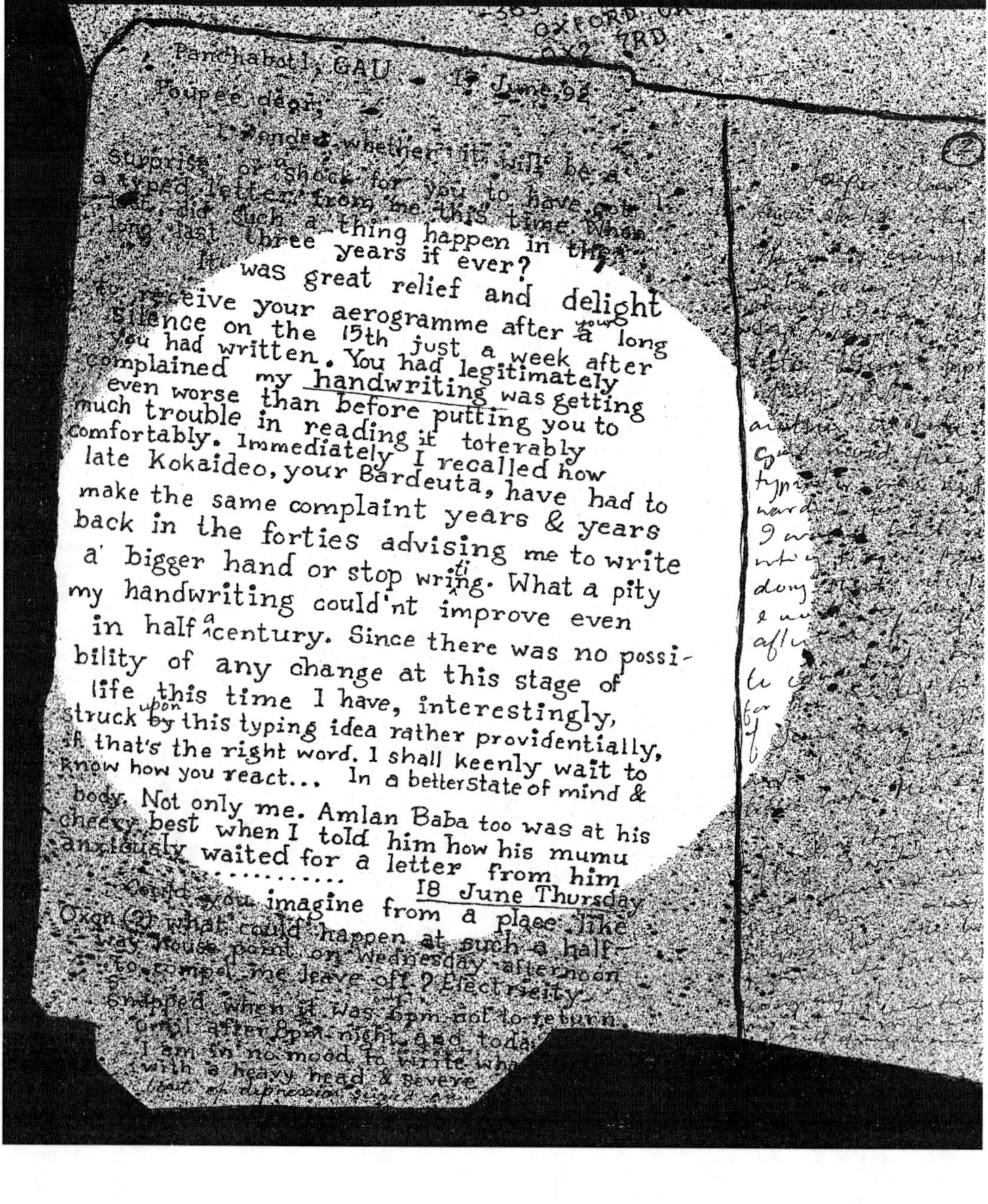

OXFORD OX
OX2 7RD

Panchabati, GAU
17 June 92

Poupee dear,

I wonder whether it will be a surprise or a shock for you to have a typed letter from me this time. When last did such a thing happen in these long last three years if ever?

It was great relief and delight to receive your aerogramme after your long silence on the 15th just a week after you had written. You had legitimately complained my handwriting was getting even worse than before putting you to much trouble in reading it tolerably comfortably. Immediately I recalled how late Kokaideo, your Bardeuta, have had to make the same complaint years & years back in the forties advising me to write a bigger hand or stop writing. What a pity my handwriting could'nt improve even in half a century. Since there was no possibility of any change at this stage of life this time I have, interestingly, struck upon this typing idea rather providentially, if that's the right word. I shall keenly wait to know how you react... In a better state of mind & body. Not only me. Amlan Baba too was at his cheeky best when I told him how his mumu anxiously waited for a letter from him ....

18 June Thursday

Could you imagine from a place like Oxon (?) what could happen at such a half-way house point on Wednesday afternoon to compel me leave off? Electricity snapped when it was 5pm not to return until after 8pm night and today I am in no mood to write what with a heavy head & severe bout of depression

Dzongri Dzongri
That's his pet. Once we reached, Capt D played with Dzongri briefly, before locking himself up with the diaries.
गुरुवार/THURSDAY
शुक्रवार/FRIDAY
4 जनवरी/JANUARY
Hours later... the door opened. Capt D came out looking for something.
need some light?
don't worry FOUND IT!

THE EXORCISM OF EMILY ROSE
1985

P. Das
D
rmal Psy.
SE BE
ED AND
FOR YOUR
TURN
I returned home the next day. Left the diaries with Capt D
WE BUY OLD NEWSPAPER, BOOKS AND MAGAZIN
He looks so familiar. HALF SMILE quick!
The bus dropped me at the highway. I started walking...
KURT VONNEGUT
God Bless You Dr. Kevorkian
Then you reach home, find a book under the door, pop a pill. Hit the bed.
But what happened to the diaries?
I haven't seen Capt D after that night

I did doctor.
I called him several times.
Phone? ya you must've called him.
But Capt D didn't answer. Not even once!
TRiiiNG
TRiiiNG
PHONE BOOK

AXA 3295
BOW WOW WOW GRRR GRR..
DAMN!
Grrr BOOOW WOW WOW
Tring Tring

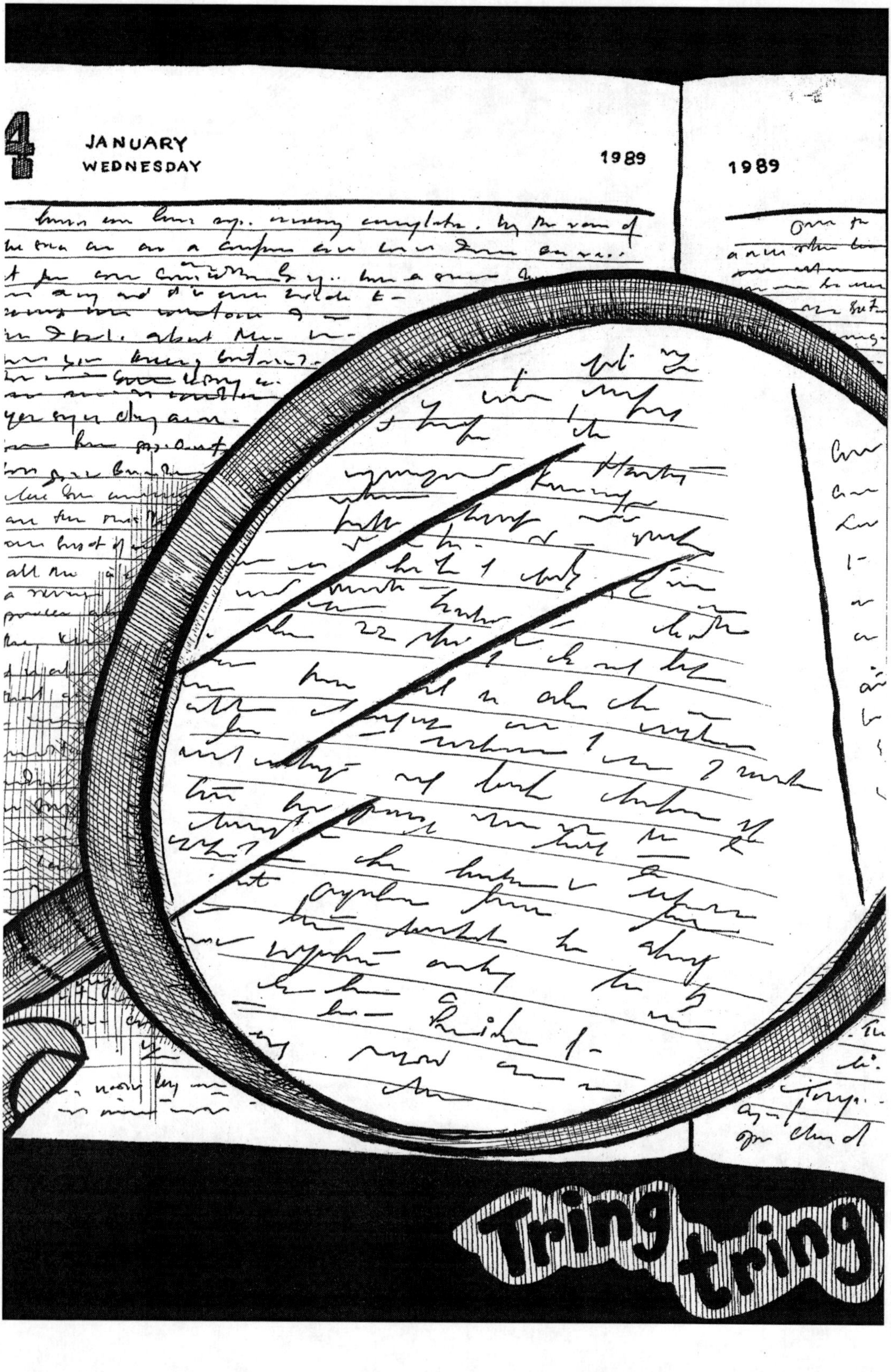
4
JANUARY
WEDNESDAY
1989
1989
Tring tring

That made me think of this Paris Review intervi-ew in which your dad said
"I have two daughters who are as talented as [my sister] was, and both of them are damned if...
Trring
Trriing
they are going to lose their poise and sense of humor by snatching up their talents and desperately running as far and as fast as they can. They saw me run as fast as I could — and it must have looked like quite a crazy performance to them.
And this is the worst possible metaphor, for what they actually saw was a man sitting still for decades.[18]

BIG BERTHA
420

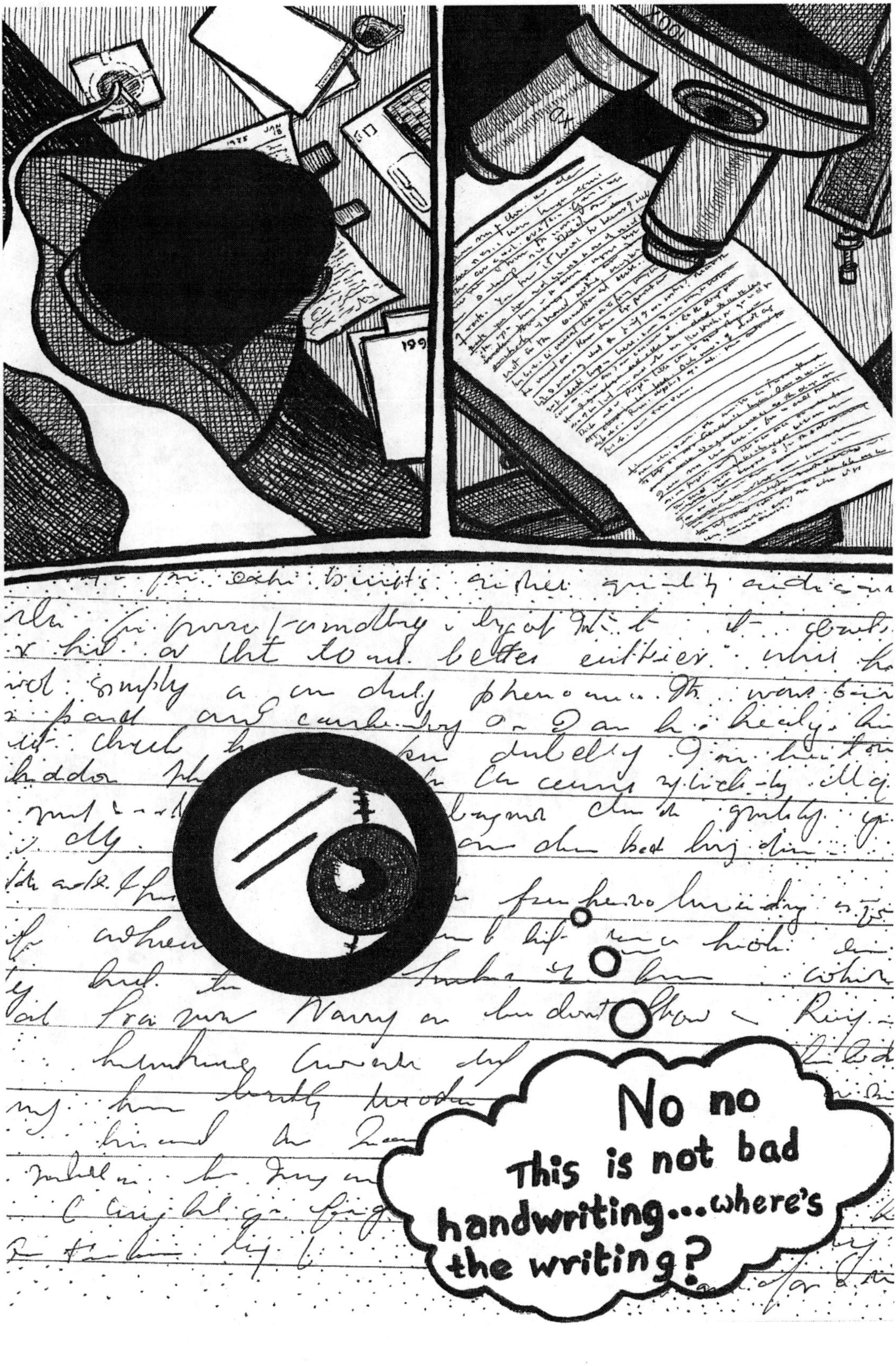
No no
This is not bad handwriting...where's the writing?

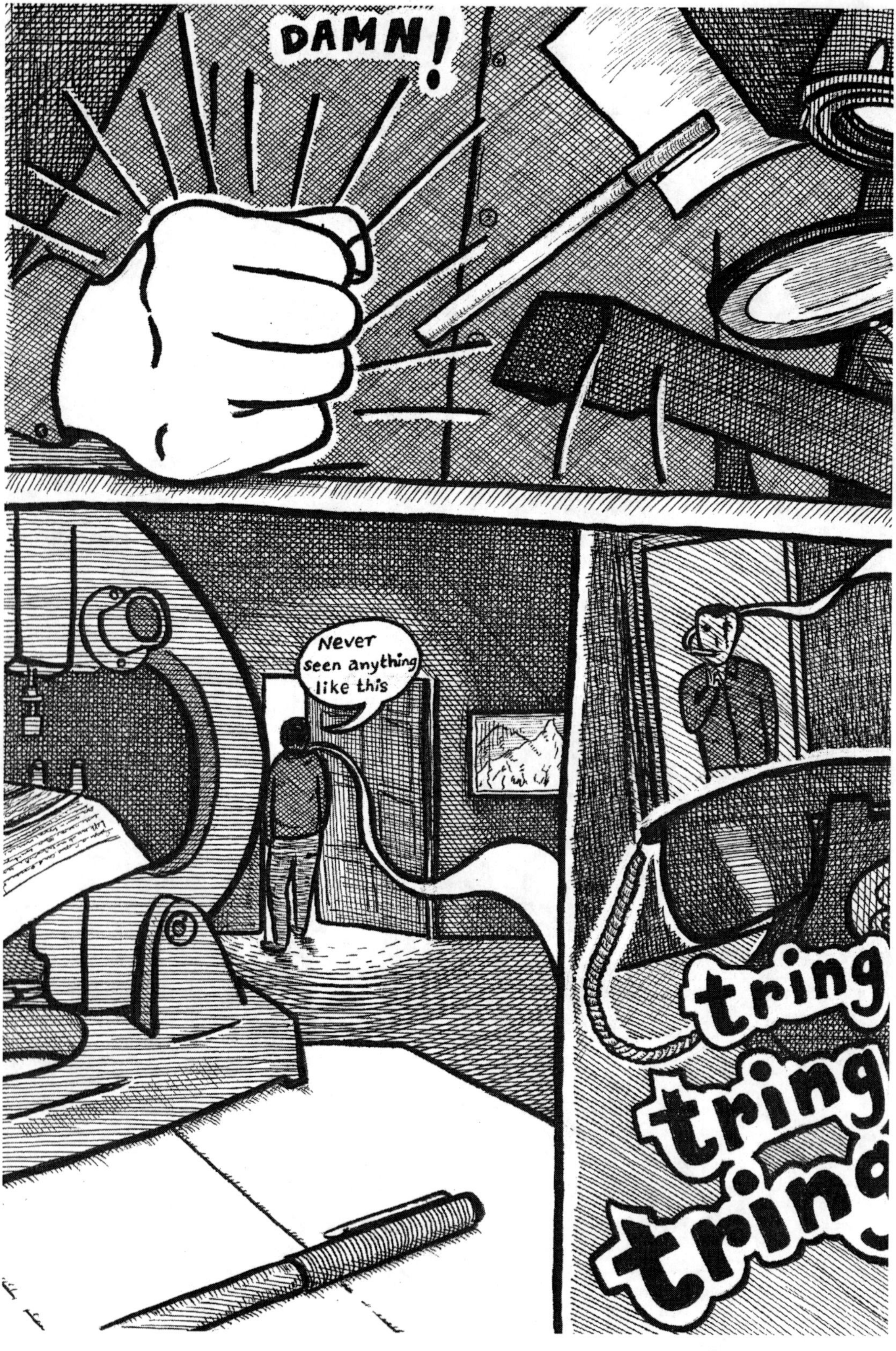
DAMN!
Never seen anything like this
tring
tring
tring

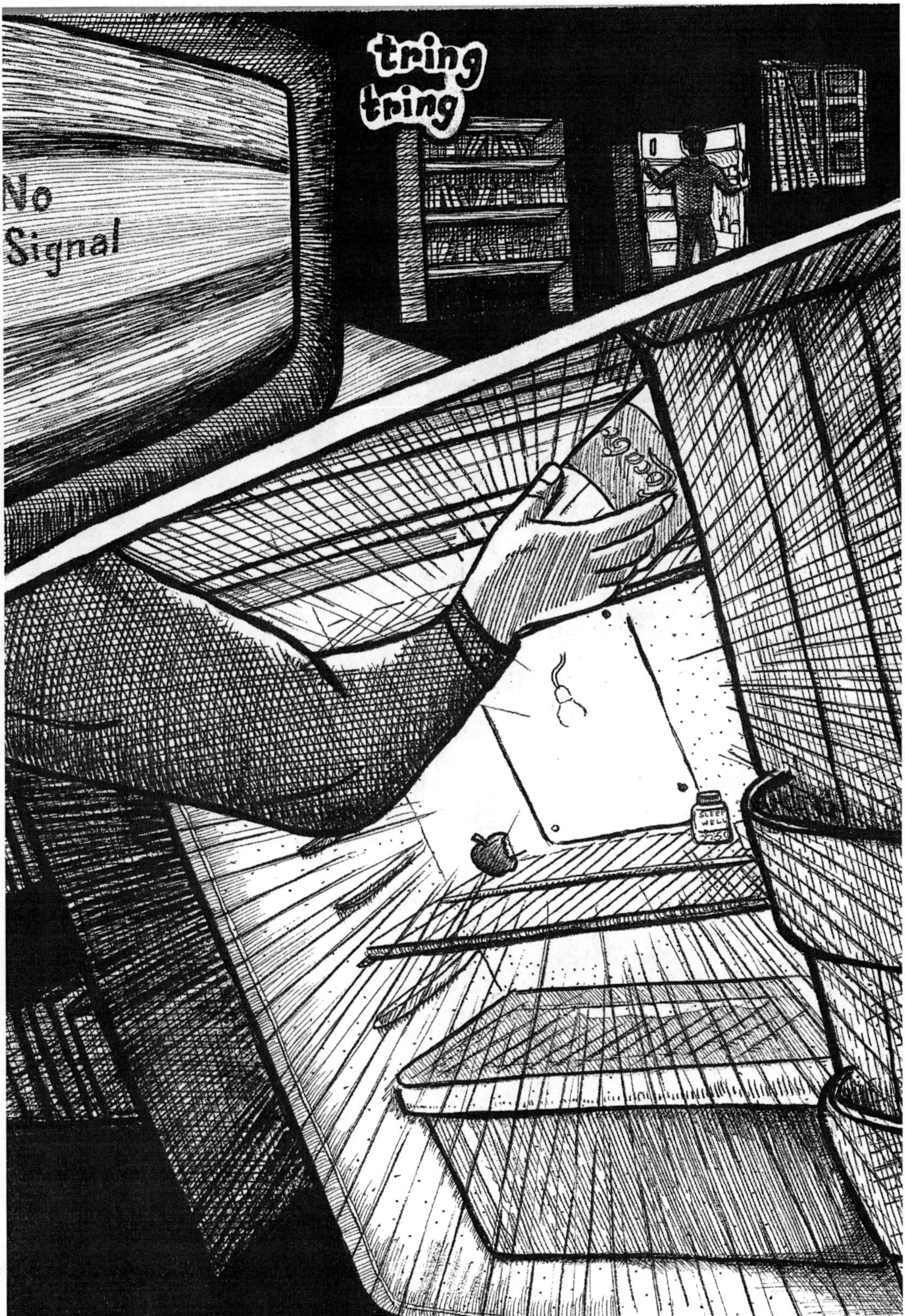
tring
tring
No
Signal

So I begin the New Year 1988 on not a very literally heavy note,
getting up later than usual, little confused about priorities and
uncertain of the future.
Yet it should … normal happy year beginning on a sacred
Friday, the day … d Gandhi's assassination – a day which
I have always ta… apart. I begin this new diary gotten
on the last day … sturday. (with nobody to remember).
Proper the begin… with Gandhi's hymn…

7 DEAD END

SOON...
RUM
YEARS BLENDED
RUM

MY DIARIES!
4 JAN
1988
1988
18 JAN

30 JAN
1988
What did I write here?

NEED HELP!
THIS IS A MESS.
THIS IS BAD.

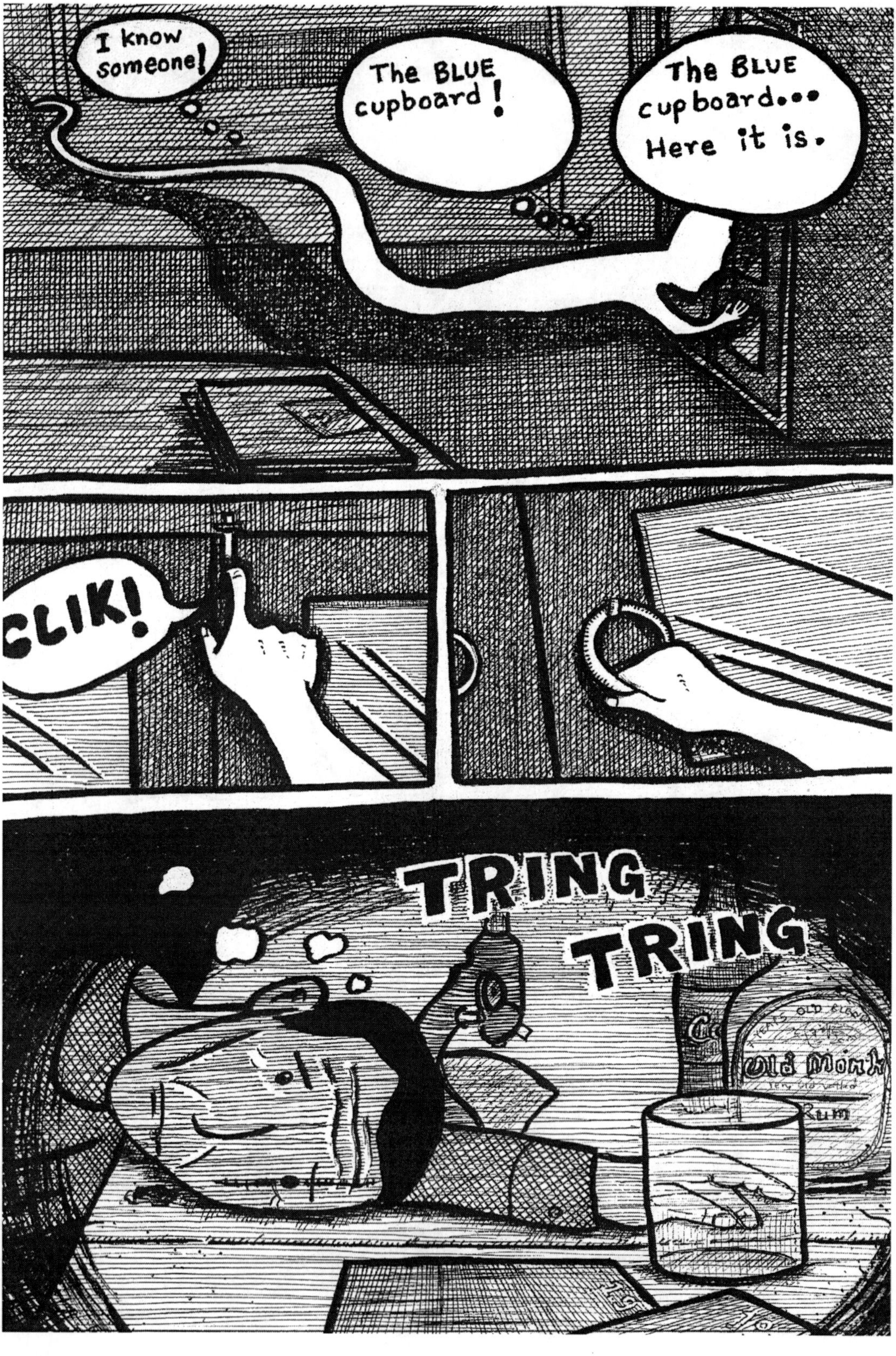
I know someone!
The BLUE cupboard!
The BLUE cupboard... Here it is.
CLIK!
TRING
TRING
Old Monk
Rum

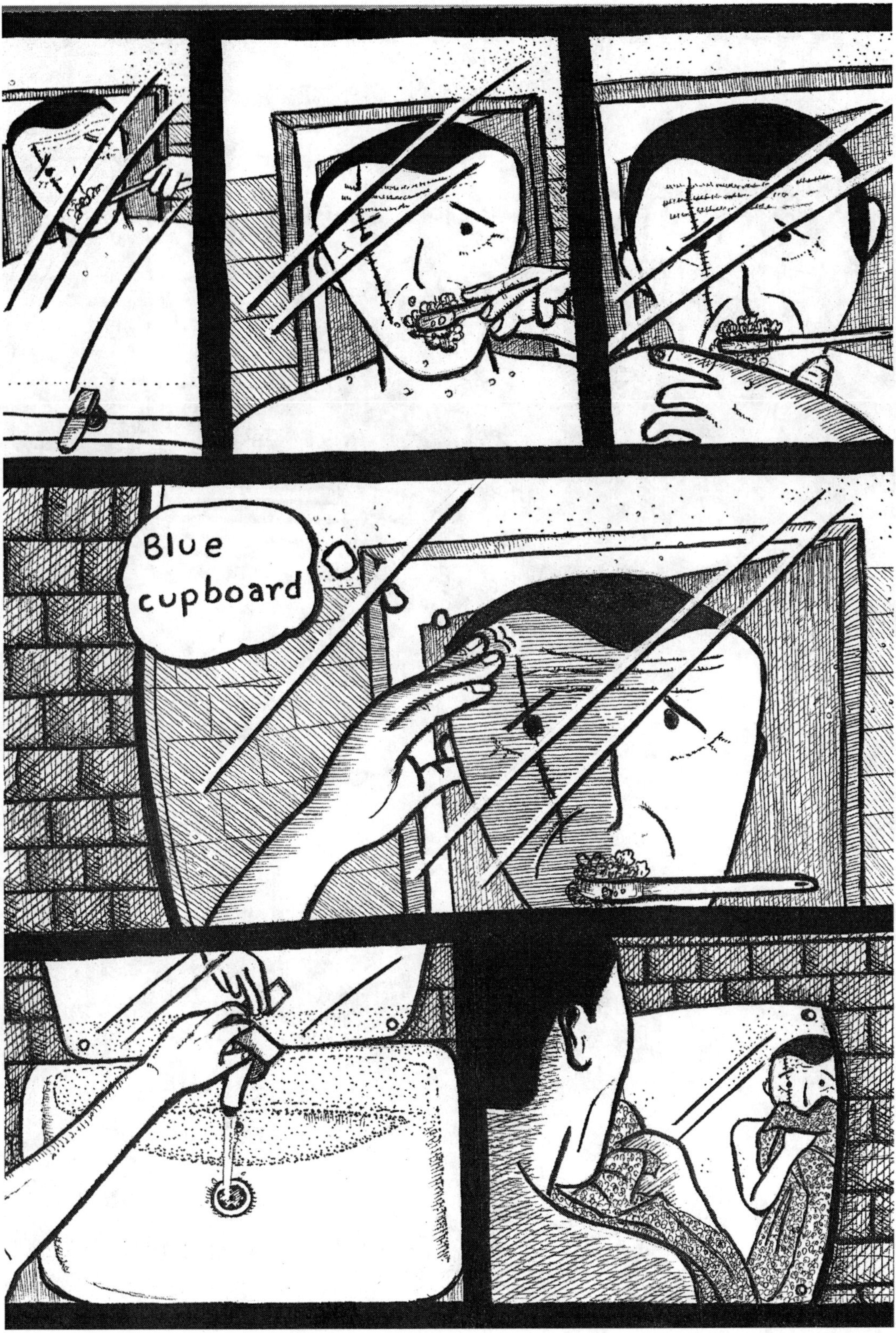
Blue
cupboard

these are my father's diaries
that BLUE cupboard!

MUNIN BARKOTOKI
SILPUKHURI
GUWAHATI

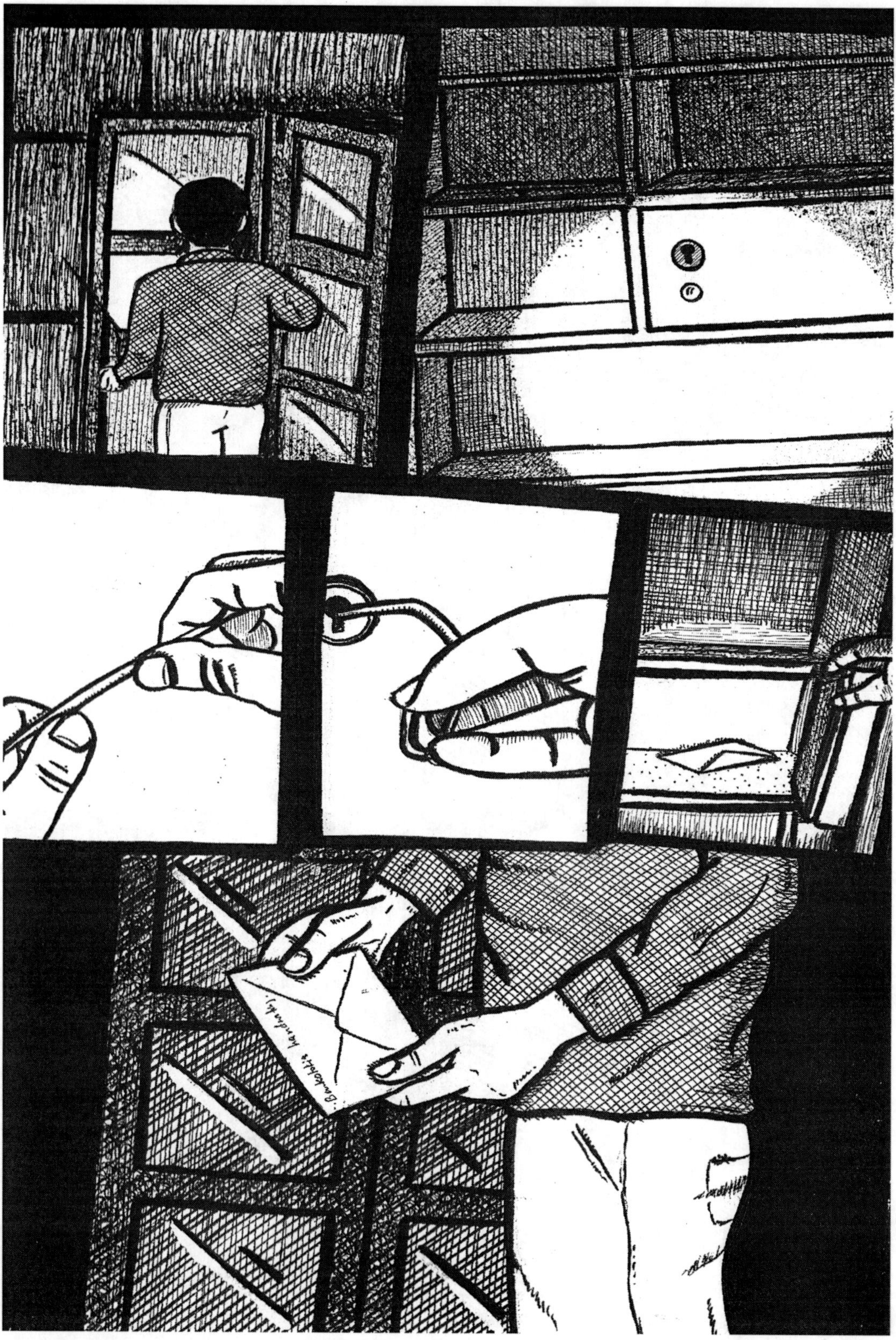

SCREECH
CaptD
Barkotoki Sir[19]
the blue blooded Assamese thinker
(Contd from page 3)
one more fact that many
may or may not know that
Sir had a very bad handwr-
iting – microscopic, illegible
and mere lines and dots.
On top of that his sentences
climbed upward when he
wrote. No newspaper or
magazine could ever publish
his handwritten articles
correctly. With time a
couple of pundits emerged
in Guwahati, with expertise
on his handwriting. Amongst
them, is the author of this
article and the other was
.
At times when Barkotoki
sir couldn't read his own
writing he'd ask us
"Look what did I write here?"
DAMN!
Tell me their names
You tricked me!
Ha ha ha

FIND HIS NUMBER
THAT'S OUR ONLY CHANCE!
YOU KNOW WHO
Here you are!
Tut Tut
TUT
Tut tut
Hello!

8 ACROSS THE BLUE TUNNEL

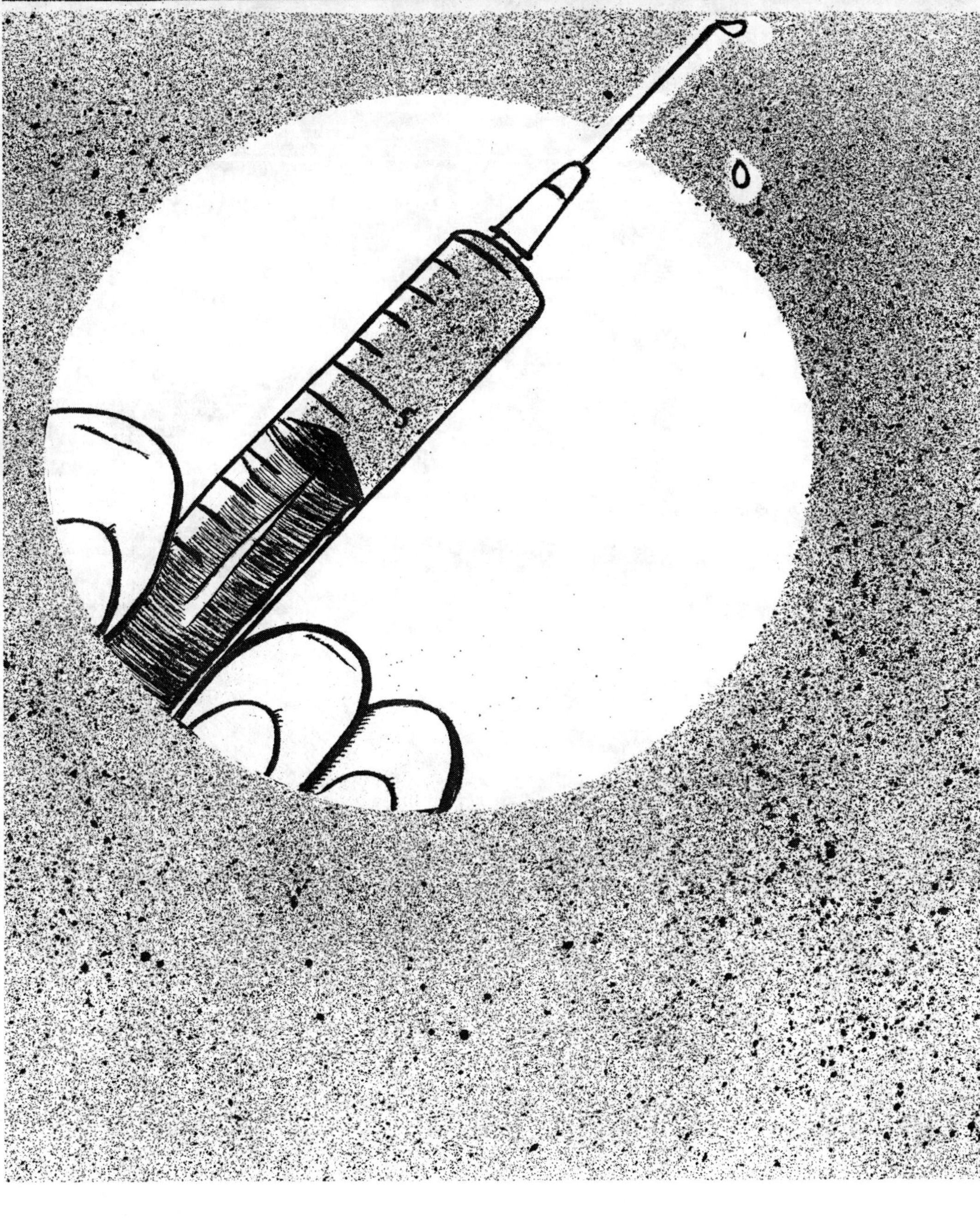

Dr P. Das
MD
Abnormal Psy
I called Capt D everyday. But I didn't hear from him.
After the 2nd week, I decided to go and see him in person.
TRING
TRING
pt D

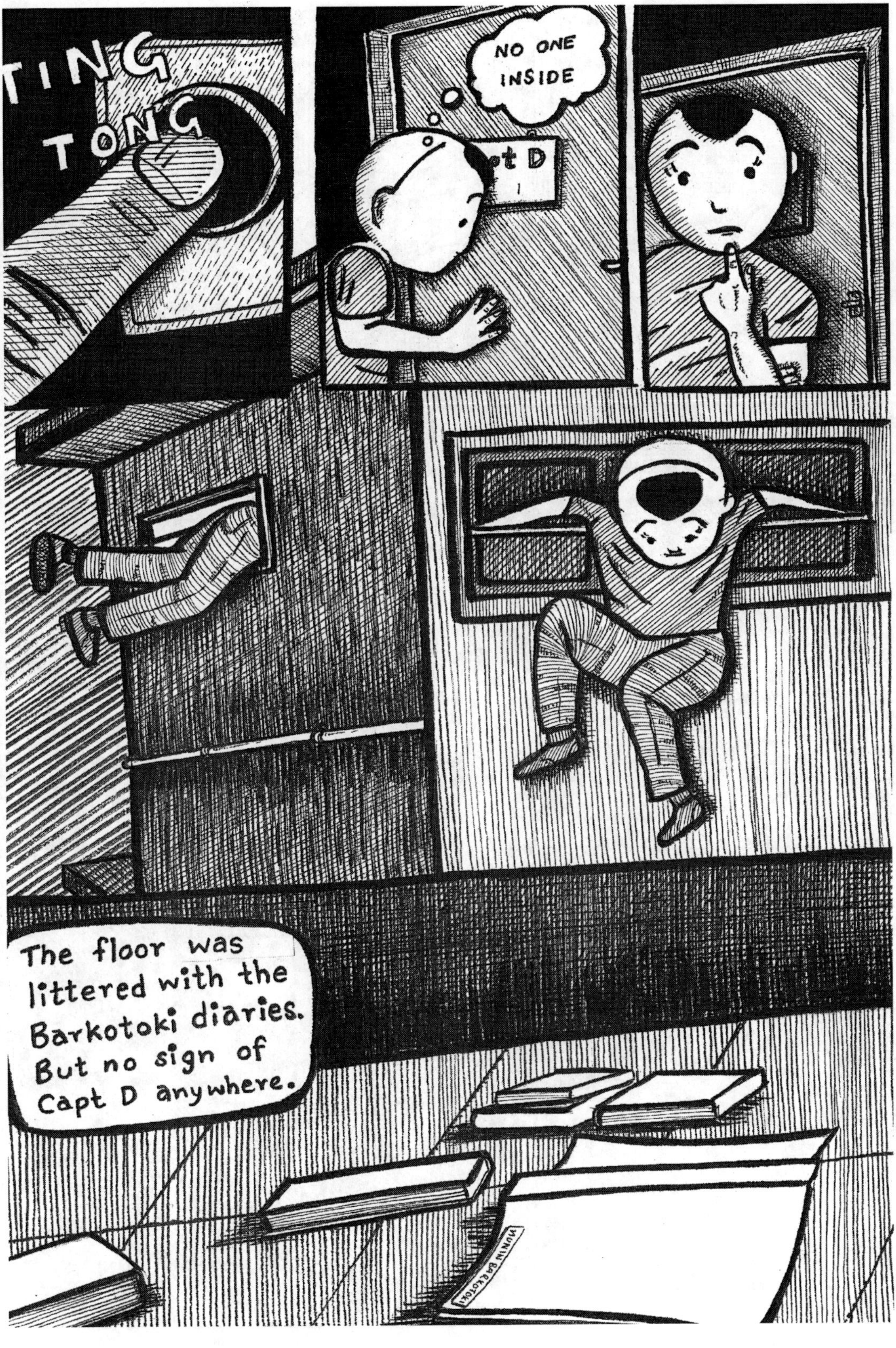
TING TONG
NO ONE INSIDE
The floor was littered with the Barkotoki diaries. But no sign of Capt D anywhere.
MUNIN BARKOTOKI

Dzongri
Dzongri
NO SIGN OF HIS DOG EITHER
hmm
SCRUFF
SCRUF
zero
Scurrrr
one
Scurr

Tring
Tring
TRING
LETHAL INJECTION FACILITY
Hello Doctor Kevorkian's office
CLIK!
Office of Dr Kevorkian

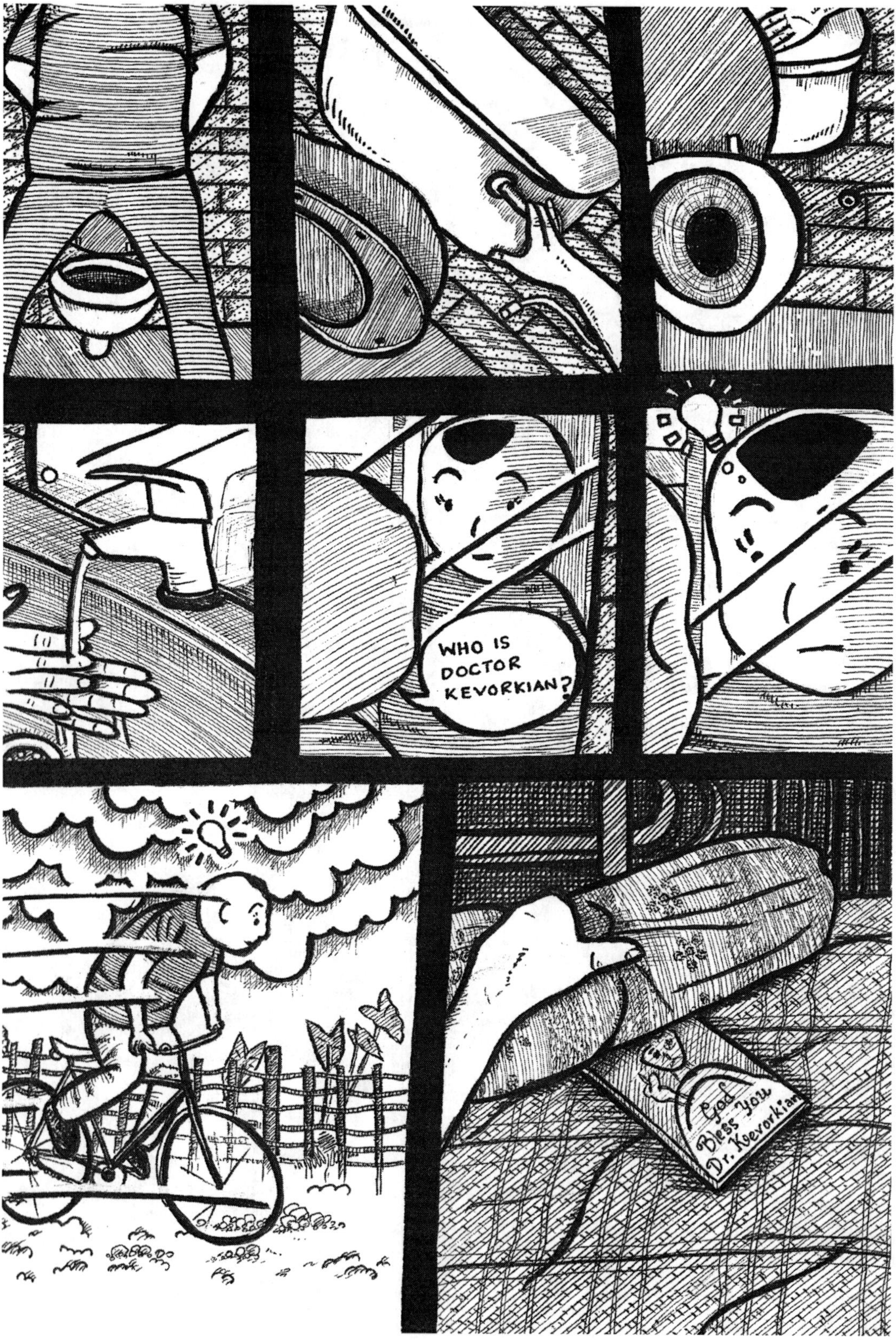
WHO IS DOCTOR KEVORKIAN?
God Bless You Dr. Kevorkian

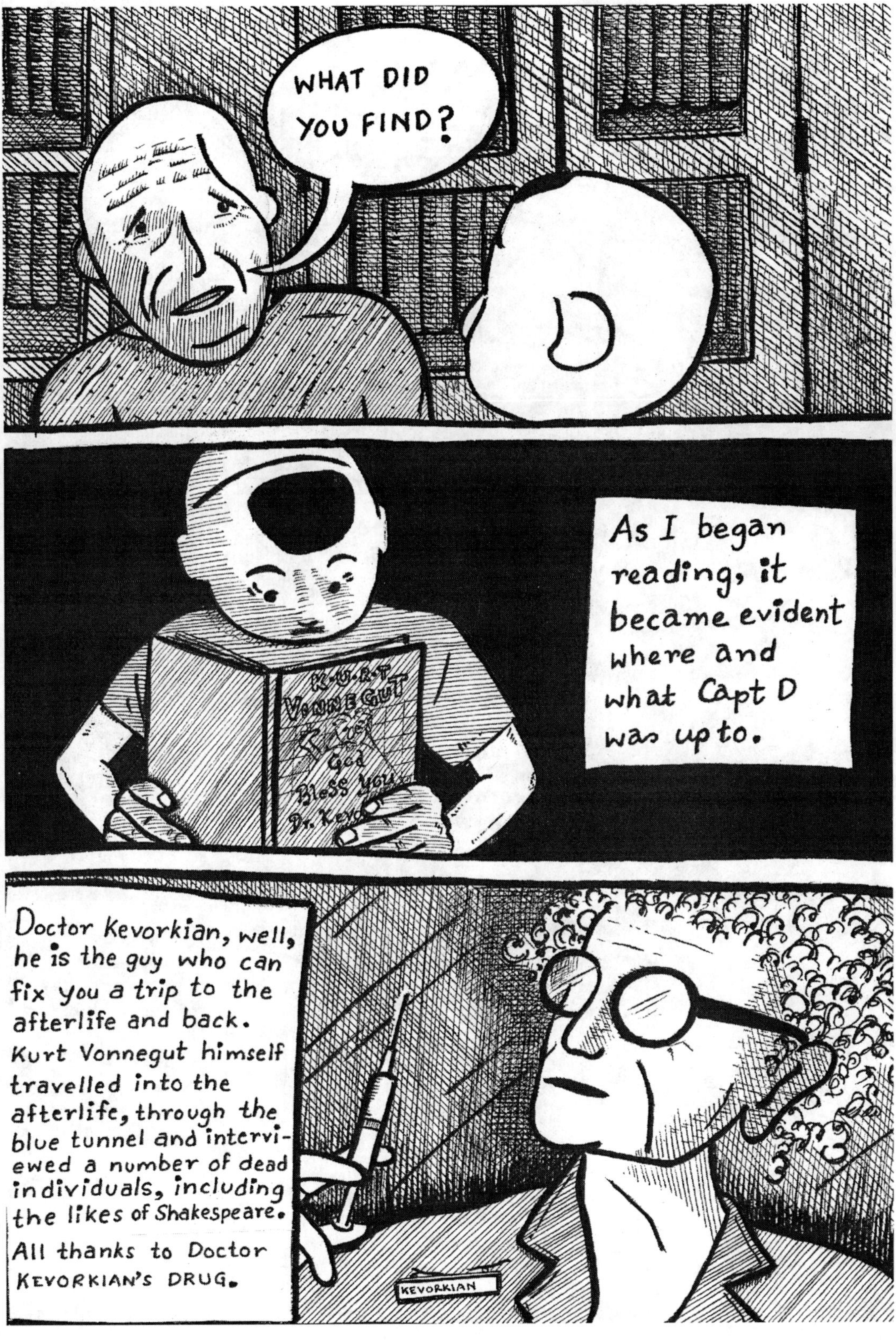
WHAT DID YOU FIND?
As I began reading, it became evident where and what Capt D was up to.
KURT VONNEGUT
God Bless You Dr. Kevo
Doctor Kevorkian, well, he is the guy who can fix you a trip to the afterlife and back. Kurt Vonnegut himself travelled into the afterlife, through the blue tunnel and interviewed a number of dead individuals, including the likes of Shakespeare.
All thanks to Doctor KEVORKIAN'S DRUG.
KEVORKIAN

ATTENTION PLEASE! THIS IS THE FIN
YELLOW CAB
Like I said Sir we haven't let anyone through in the last one year. Legal issues.
But the last call he made was to your number
We don't keep a record. Sir you've to leave now.
DZONGRI!
WOOF WOOF

Dzongri, where's Capt D?
BOW WOW
STOP STOP!
YOU ARE FREAKING ME OUT
Grrr Grrr
UNGODLY INTERVIEW

1. KEVORKIAN DRUG
2. CAR KEY
3. Very hard to find a Right Hand drive. It's an old car, but should get you through.
4. PUMP THE BRAKES
See you!
Capt D
MEET
1. Late Arun Sarma (playwright)
Late Krishna Bhuya
(MB's friend)
3. Late Satyen Barkataki
(MB's elder brother)
Dzongri
Let's go!
VROOOM
VROOM

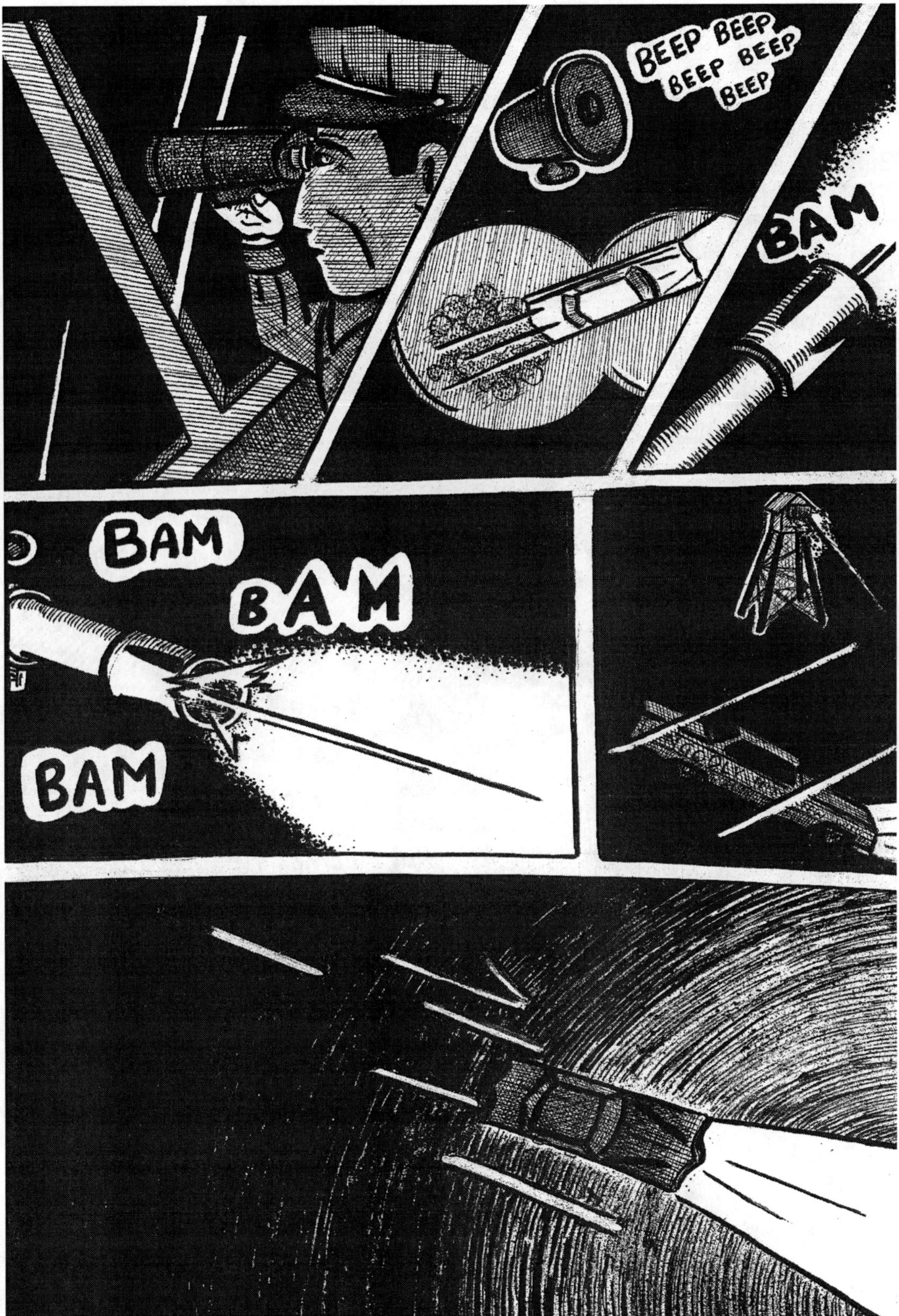
BEEP BEEP
BEEP BEEP
BEEP
BAM
BAM
BAM
BAM

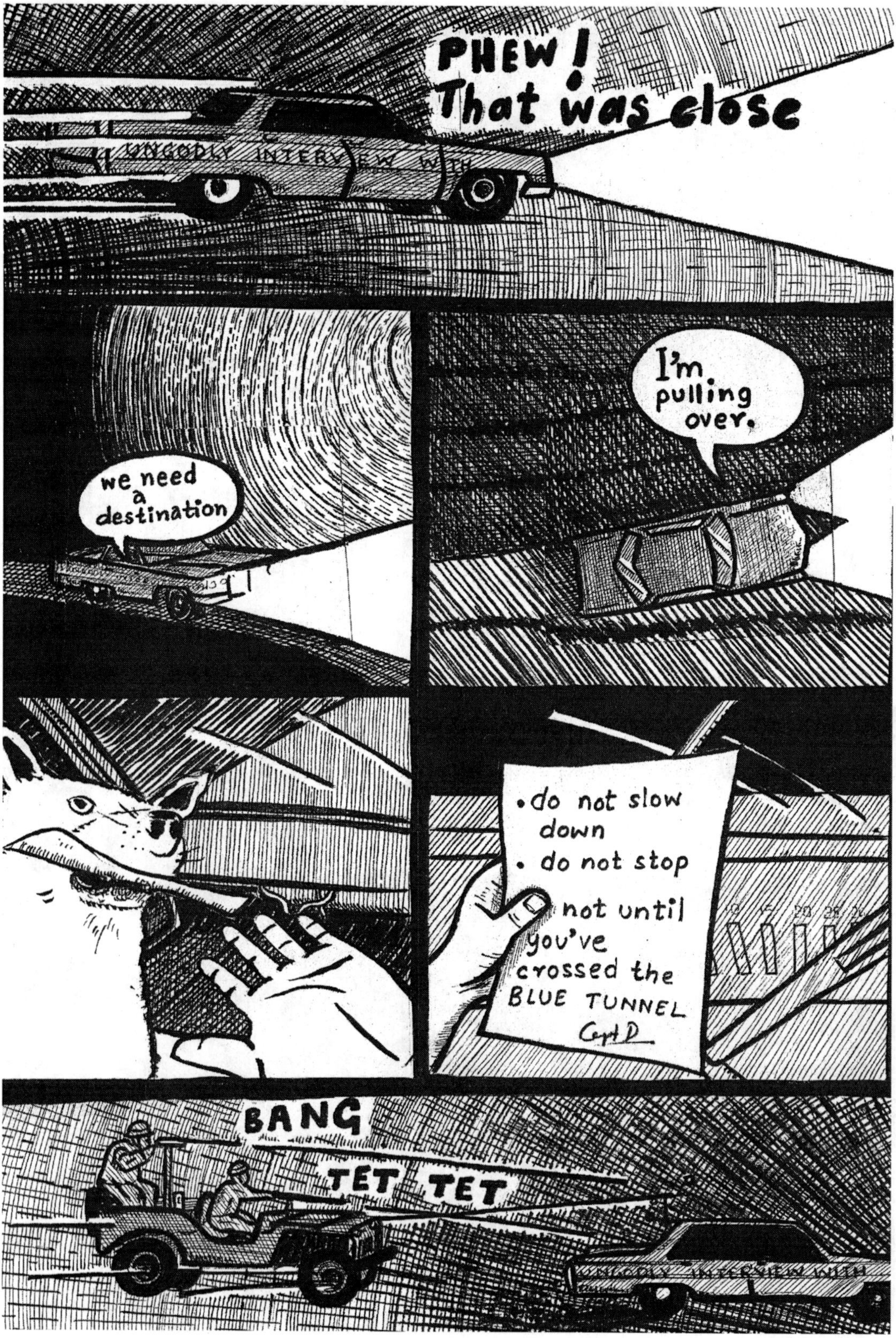
PHEW! That was close
we need a destination
I'm pulling over.
• do not slow down
• do not stop
not until you've crossed the BLUE TUNNEL
Capt D
BANG
TET TET

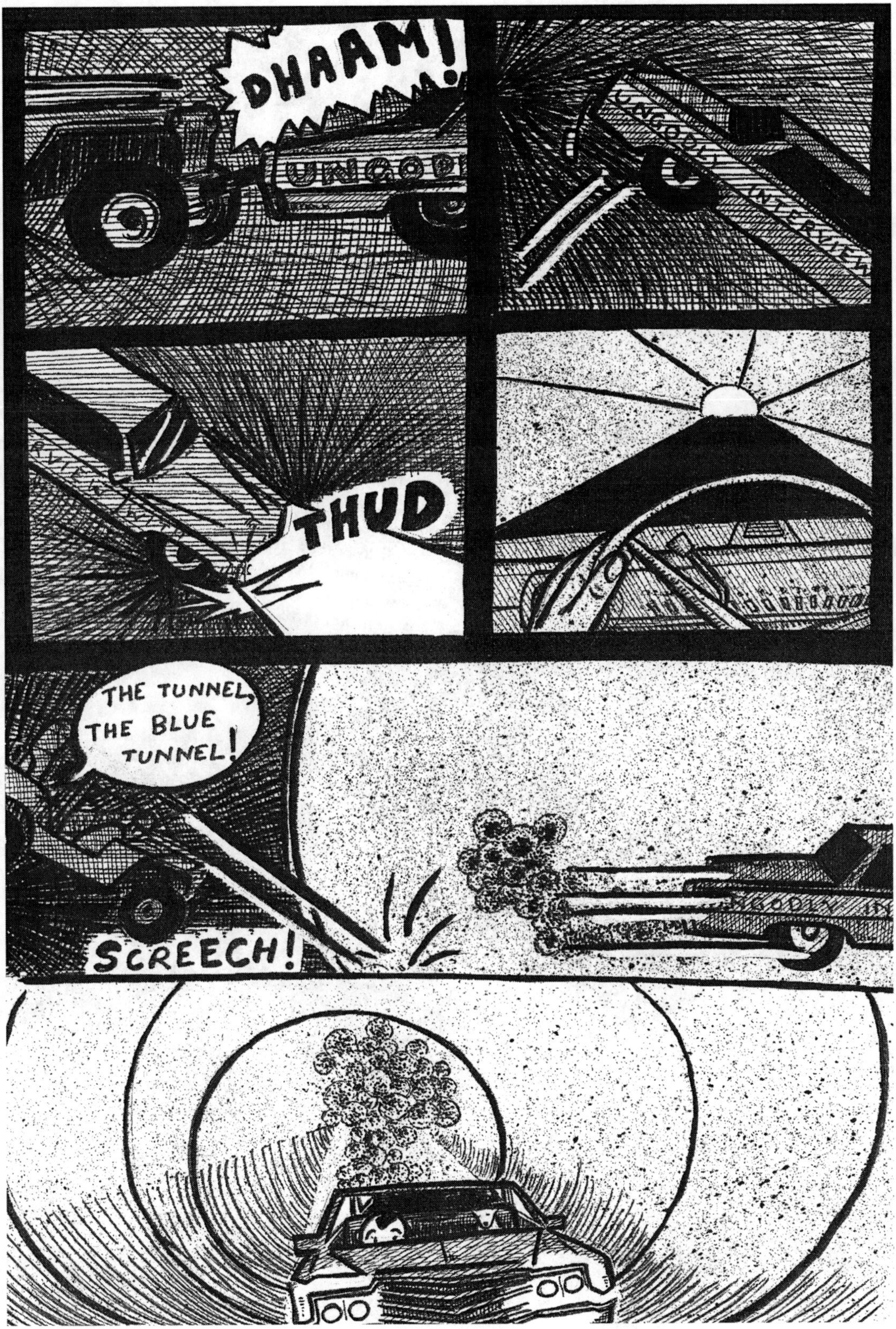
DHAAM!
UNGODLY INTERVIEW
THUD
THE TUNNEL, THE BLUE TUNNEL!
SCREECH!

9 AN UNGODLY INTERVIEW

VROOM
we need to stop
DAMN
UNGODLY
BRILLIANT!
Dzongri you almost got us killed
We are not going anywhere unless you tell me EVERYTHING
Well don't speak. Be my guest
Absolutely NO HURRY. You are strange
khrr
khrr
KRISHN

CHILDHOOD
I want to see Barkotoki's childhood
KRISHNA BHUYAN
UNGOOLY INTERV WITH
KRISHNA BHUYAN
TRING!
CHILDHOOD
UNGOOLY INTERVIEW WITH
KRISHNA BHUYAN

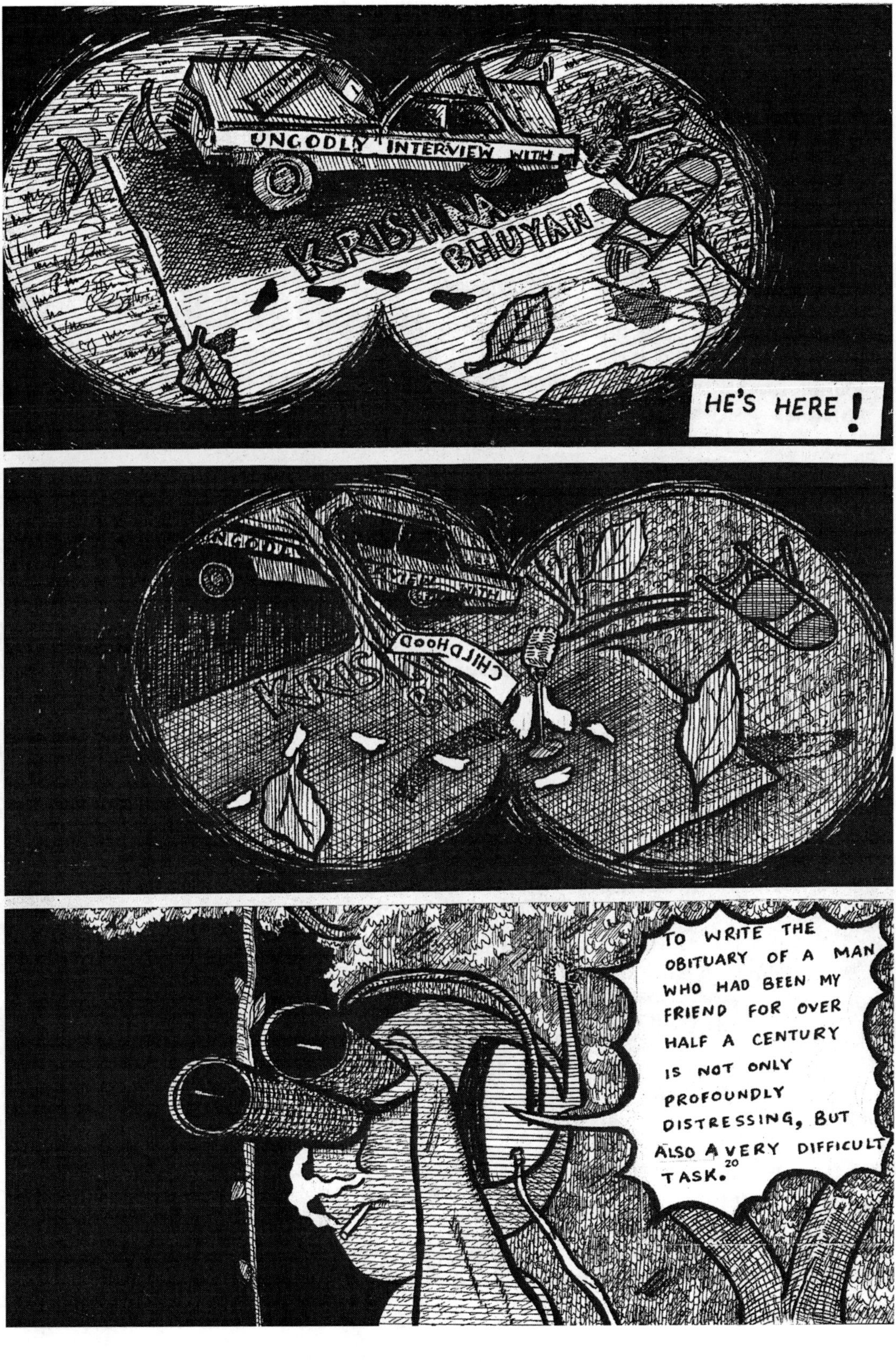
UNGODLY INTERVIEW WITH
KRISHNA
BHUYAN
HE'S HERE!
CHILDHOOD
TO WRITE THE OBITUARY OF A MAN WHO HAD BEEN MY FRIEND FOR OVER HALF A CENTURY IS NOT ONLY PROFOUNDLY DISTRESSING, BUT ALSO A VERY DIFFICULT TASK.[20]

Very difficult. These are some photographs that I'd kept aside after Munin died in 1993. Munin Barkotoki was the youngest child of Raisaheb Durgadhar Barkotoki.
In 1921, during the non cooperation movement, Raisaheb quit his School inspector's job and moved to Calcutta.
Raisaheb had moved to Calcutta to open a printing press.
In 1930 when I was in IXth at the Jorhat Govt. High School...
That year Raisaheb returned. And Munin became my CLASSMATE.
That's him
Fresh from his Calcutta background, Munin was shy. As luck would have it, we sat on the same bench. And as I became familiar with Munin, I discovered his habit of reading! Reading books, magazines and newspapers EVERYDAY!

In Calcutta he must have read lots of books in Bengali literature. He surprised me by the sweep of his KNOWLEDGE, about books by the great Bengali writers like Tagore, Bankim Chatterjee, Saratchandra, Bibhutibhusan, Ashapurna Devi, Buddhadev Bose, Tarashankar and others...
Soon we were promoted to Class X.
SHNA
BHUYAN
UNGODLY INTERVIEW WITH KRISHNA BHUYAN.
• Reads
• Knowledge sweep of

Munin I'm thinking of bringing out a lit magazine
Handwritten? Excellent. You start. I'll follow.
STD.X
Friends, I bring to you 'Kumudini'!
Kumudini
NEXT MONTH...
Friends, I bring to you 'Ārati'!
Ārati
Ārati was received with acclaim when circulated. After we'd produced 6 or 7 issues, Munin wrote an editorial in Ārati criticizing the British for hanging the patriot and revolutionary of Bengal...
...named, if I remember alright, Dinesh Gupta. Someone brought this to the notice of the school authority...
Ārati
Seize everything and burn it.
SEDITION
THIS IS SEDITION!
All our issues with their back-numbers were seized and destroyed and we were both sternly warned not to bring out the magazine any more.
And, that WAS THE BEGINNING of our LITERARY ACTIVITIES directed and destined to accomplish some positive results, notwithstanding the initial damper.

During this time Raisaheb passed away, leaving his wife Kamalini Devi, heartbroken.
Our houses were only a kilometre apart. Munin spent most of his leisure time with us...
Truth is, after the death of her husband, Munin's mother suffered from a melancholic dejection and withdrew herself in her shell of reveries.
With his brother Satyen Barkotoki away from home at his post, his two elder sisters married off, Munin did not have much company at home.
BURMA
That's Satyen
Meanwhile
We passed the Matriculation exam in 1932 and the I.A. examination of the Calcutta University in 1934, and DECIDED to join the Cotton College for higher studies.
UNGODLY INTERVIEW WITH KRISHNA BHUYAN
• Reads
• Patriotic
• Lonely?

We found a new, near perfect arrangement – a mess with a separate room of our own AND a cook to serve us meals.
After about 6-7 weeks, one afternoon we returned to our mess early. We looked for Gouri, the mess cook, to get some tea.
The kitchen door was locked from inside. It was a bamboo door with holes. We peeped through it and were aghast to see Gouri swinging an axe and shouting at some imaginary person. Gouri, a big muscular man was apparently a raving mad man. We ran for our lives.

That evening Munin went to his aunt's home at Panchabati Ashram in Silpukhuri and I to my cousin's at Uzanbazar, and told them the frightful story.

Neither Munin's aunt, nor my cousin allowed us to return to the mess.

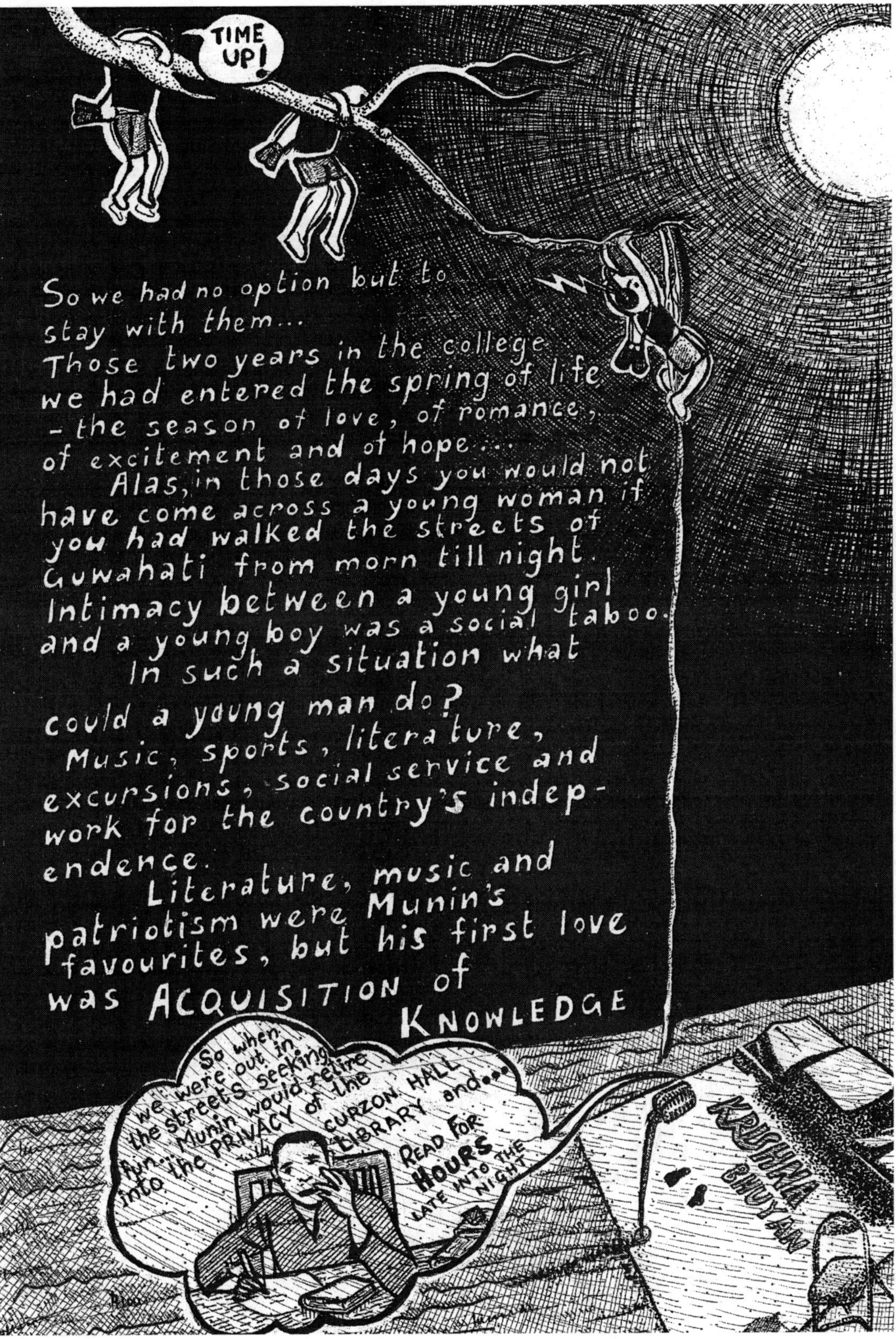
TIME UP!
So we had no option but to stay with them...
Those two years in the college we had entered the spring of life - the season of love, of romance, of excitement and of hope...
Alas, in those days you would not have come across a young woman if you had walked the streets of Guwahati from morn till night. Intimacy between a young girl and a young boy was a social taboo.
In such a situation what could a young man do?
Music, sports, literature, excursions, social service and work for the country's independence.
Literature, music and patriotism were Munin's favourites, but his first love was ACQUISITION of KNOWLEDGE
So when we were out in the streets seeking fun... Munin would retire into the PRIVACY of the CURZON HALL LIBRARY and... READ FOR HOURS LATE INTO THE NIGHT
KRISHNA BHUYAN

BHUYAN
During this time Munin accomplished something substantial in the literary field. His short stories were published in Āwāhan and Jayanti, and were well received.
Munin got the highest marks in the preliminary internals. But a couple of months before the B.A. final exam, one afternoon...
Krishna! I am dropping out of the exams
Are you crazy!
Think of your future!
I am not prepared
DRINK YOUR TEA!
After some introspection..
and cups and cups of tea!
Munin you are right
Even I am not prepared
What did I tell you!
AND...
What fun!
Munin went to Dacca
I left for Chittagong
Sometime in 1938, after 2 years of wandering we came across each other in Jorhat and...
We've blundered
You're right
Let's take the exam
At the long last sat for the exam
Munin was surprised!
He stood 1st among the distinguished graduates and won the gold medal.
A PECULIAR TRAIT
"Munin did not lack self confidence. But he was always after some imaginary perfection. This peculiar trait led him to quit writing short stories despite initial success. He repeated himself in 1941- he dropped out of his M.A. exam...
In our middle age, I pointed out to him that all the Knowledge he had so assiduously gathered had been of no use to him, "no fame no fortune" Munin greeted me with a sardonic smile, "you mean creative work of permanent value! like Hamlet of Shakespeare fifth symphony of Bethoveen, well well why not do something like that yourself?" So that was all there was to it?"

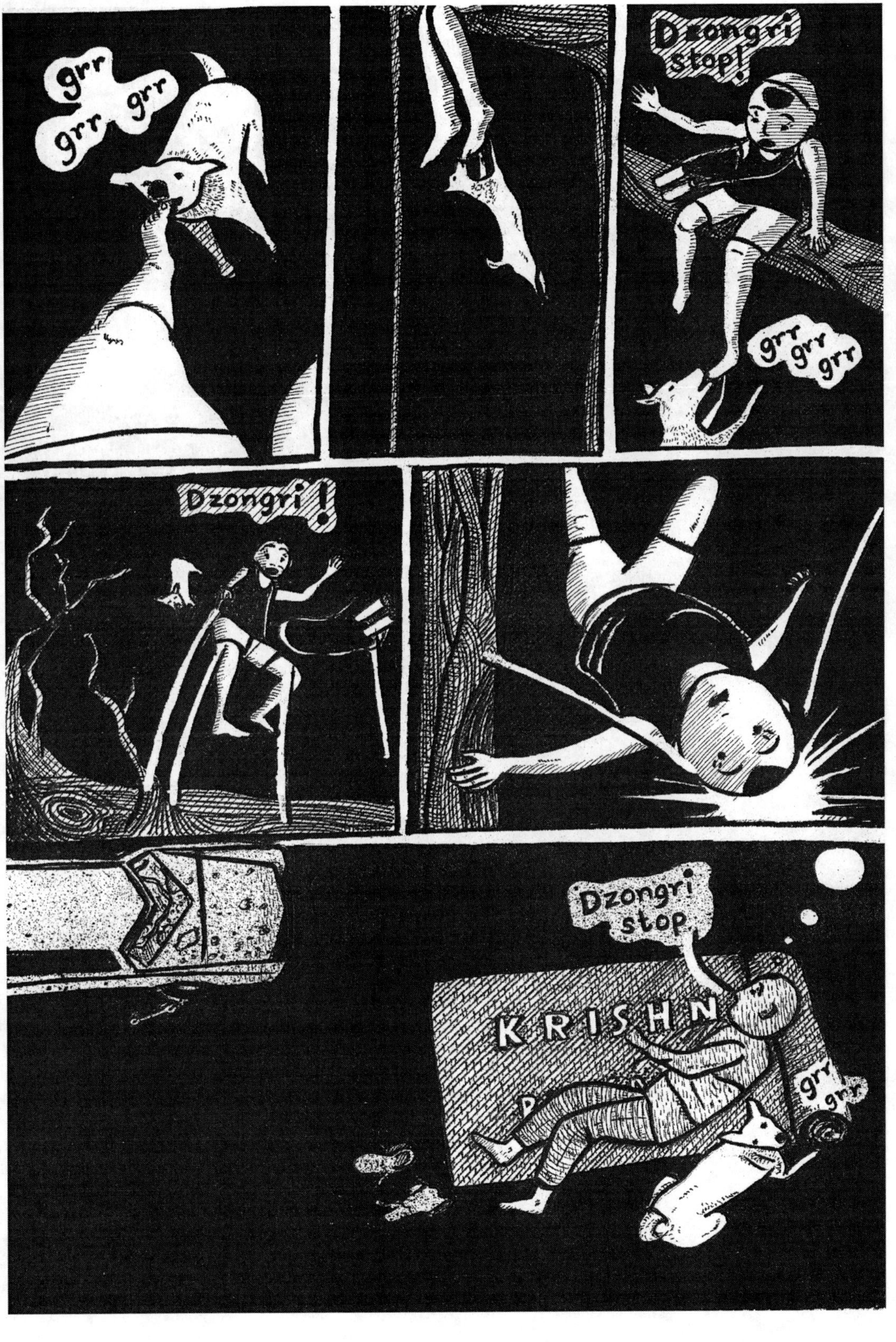
grr grr grr
Dzongri stop!
grr grr grr
Dzongri!
Dzongri stop
KRISHN
grr grr

10 GHOST of a MAGISTRATE

ISHN
DICTIONARY
TRANSLATE THIS
VROOM VROOM
I'M GOING TO FIND YOU

SATYENDRANATH BARKATAKI AND HIS PRIVATE LIBRARY
On the 15th of Sep 2012, an article appeared in the PURBANCHAL by Dr. Bandita Goswami Saikia. Titled 'Book: Private Libraries' the article talks about several private libraries, including the library of
Satyen Barkataki, a retired Govt. official who came to live at Titabar in Melamati. The article reveals how a chunk of many of his valuable books were recovered from a cart puller by luck, who was on his way to dispose them off.
Satyen Barkataki's death occured suddenly in 1984 in Calcutta. I had been to his library in Shillong... To figure out the whereabouts of the rest of his books, it would be prudent to seek the cart puller's help.[21]
ASSAMESE ENGLISH DICTIONARY
SATYEN BARKATAKI WHERE ARE YOU?

HELLO. LOOKING. FOR. ME?
KEEP. DRIVING. DO. NOT. STOP.
THE ESCAPADES OF A MAGISTRATE
NOW. WHERE. DID. YOU. FIND. THIS! Don't. LIE. to.me.
THE ESCAPADES OF A MAGISTRATE
S.BARKATAKI, I.A.S.
BEEN DRIVING FOR DAYS, LOOKING FOR YOU. NOT A SOUL. UNTIL SOMETHING APPEARED
MEET
A CART PULLER WITH A CARTLOAD OF BOOKS
?
!
THE ESCAPADES OF A MAGISTRA
S.BARKATA

WHAT. DID. YOU. DO. WITH. MY. BOOK?
I tried reading it
DID. YOU. LIKE. MY. BOOK?
I'm afraid I can't tell. Didn't read it all
people whom
across- both officials and non
I don't know why - but autobiographies seem to be a bit uncommon in India. This is the sort of literature we need most; it is both interesting and instructive and profitable to read.
I am sure that this attempt on the part of Shri Barkataki to share his experience with readers will prove successful.
Bhopal
January 13, 1961
KAILASH NATH KATJU
Chief Minister, Madhy
22
I could only read the FOREWORD. The one written by Kailash Nath Katju

DR. KAILASH. NATH. KATJU.
OH! I. REMEMBER. EVERYTHING
I used to be an ICS officer at the time when India was fighting for its INDEPENDENCE from Britain.
Independence finally came in 1947.
AIJAL
OFFICE OF THE DEPUTY COMMISSIONER, AIJAL
In 1949 I was transferred as Deputy Commissioner to one of the important hill-districts — which were till then a close preserve of Britishers. I was the first 'Kala' (black) Administrator to be put in charge of this district. Thanks to the teachings of British and other foreign missionaries, the hill-tribes looked upon the plainsman as heathens — a man from the plains was a despicable specimen of humanity, superior to them only in trickery and low cunning... But to cut a long story short, I spent four years in this district, the four happiest years of my service life...[23]
AIJAL
110 MILES
LUNGLEH
PAKISTAN
BURMA
NEED TO CONNECT LUNGLEH BY ROAD.
PARTITION DISRUPTED THE COMMERCE
THAT USED TO FLOW THROUGH RANGAMATI
BUT WHERE IS THE FUND...
SOON. I. HAD. THE. TIME. TO. STUDY. MIZO. LIFE. AT. CLOSE. QUARTERS... I. FOUND. THAT. THEY. MADE. AND. MAINTAINED. VILLAGE. ROADS... LAID. PATHWAYS. TO. JHUM. AREAS. AND. BUILT. CHURCHES. SCHOOL. AND. CLUB. HOUSES. ALL. THESE. WERE. REALLY. COMMUNITY. PROJECTS... WORKING. FOR. THE. GOOD. OF. THE. COMMUNITY. APPEARED. TO. BE. AN. INGRAINED. HABIT. WITH. THE. MIZOS.
I. WONDERED. IF. THEY. CAN. BE. PERSUADED. TO. COVER. WIDER. AREAS.
MIZOS HAVE BUILT
A ROAD THAT'S WORTH ONE CRORE
Work started on this road on the day India became a Republic. The projected road, which will be 128 miles in length, will link up Aijal, the district headquarters, with Lungleh, the southern sub-divisional town...
In the first week of January 1950 a committee of officials and non-officials with Mr. Barkataki as President was set up...
An appeal was issued urging those who lived within comparatively easy reach of the proposed road to give labour and others were asked to contribute to a special fund. When the first ceremonial sod was turned by the Rev. E.L. Mendus, of the Welsh mission, at a function near Aijal, 3000 people, many of them women, were present with pickaxes, spades and other implements carried from home. They set to work immediately the function was over.
* * *
Dr. Katju, India's Home Minister, who toured the Lushai Hills in December and drove in a jeep over the first few miles of the road, was so "tremendously impressed" by the work that at a meeting in Aijal he declared:
"Wherever I go I shall hold this up as an ideal before India."
Dr. KATJU in Aijal, 1950

But. all. these. happened. long. ago. You. on. the. other. hand. are. ALIVE
Young. man. tell. me. What. will. your. autobiography. be. like.
Never gave it a thought Sir.
Where can I find Late Munin, your brother?
you'll. find Munin. EVERY. ONE. is. here. Keep. driving. So. long.
What will my autobiography be like?

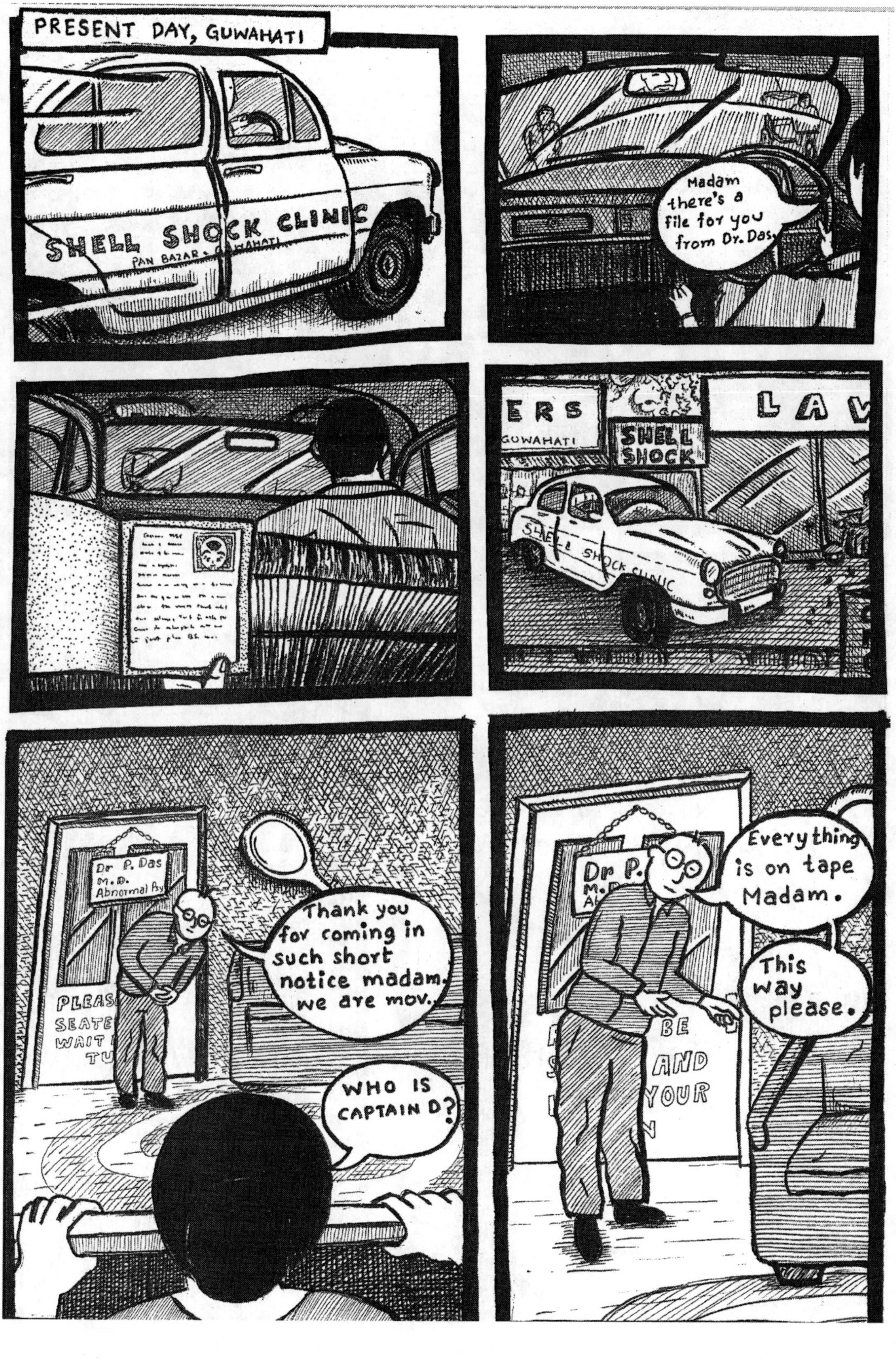
PRESENT DAY, GUWAHATI
SHELL SHOCK CLINIC
PAN BAZAR, GUWAHATI
Madam there's a file for you from Dr. Das.
ERS
GUWAHATI
SHELL SHOCK
LAW
SHELL SHOCK CLINIC
Dr P. Das M.D. Abnormal Psy
PLEAS SEATE WAIT TU
Thank you for coming in such short notice madam. we are mov..
WHO IS CAPTAIN D?
Dr P.
Everything is on tape Madam.
This way please.
BE AND YOUR

Capt D. Hmm. I didn't mention him in the file, did I? Allow me to explain.
ok ok great!
CONTROL ROOM
Check pulse and BP.
Madam we are right on time! We are meeting Capt D. Shall we?
CONTROL ROOM
This way Madam.
REM Noted over
KEVORKIAN'S DRUG

so. long.
young. man. what. will. your. autobiography. be like?
The ghost of Satyen Barkatoki vanished. I kept driving, constantly aware that the spell from Kevorkian's injection might wear out any moment.
MEET
HAAAM! Capt D where are you?
Keep going keep going
Capt D c'mon are you?
Young man what will your autobiography be like?
WHUH WHUH WHUH

FOOTNOTE

* The Hump (also Aluminium Trail) was the aerial route of the first and history's most dangerous airlift. The route was established from India's northeast via Burma into West China, when the invading Japanese cut off China from the outside world during WWII. For three and a half years Allied aircrafts supplied troops and weapons into China. It was 800 kms of the world's most treacherous route. Between 1942 to 1946 more than 600 Allied aircrafts vanished in these rugged mountains.

In 2012, when Clayton Kuhles was in India, he first heard about 'old wreckages'. In the following years he has located 22 crash sites.

SCREECH
Dzongri You gave me a SCARE!
Stop stop! Dzongri you're so DEAD I swear.
Give me the KEY
grr grr
Dzongri
grr-grr

zzzZ
KUKROO KO
KUKROO KOO
AR

No!
this can't be...
AXA 3295

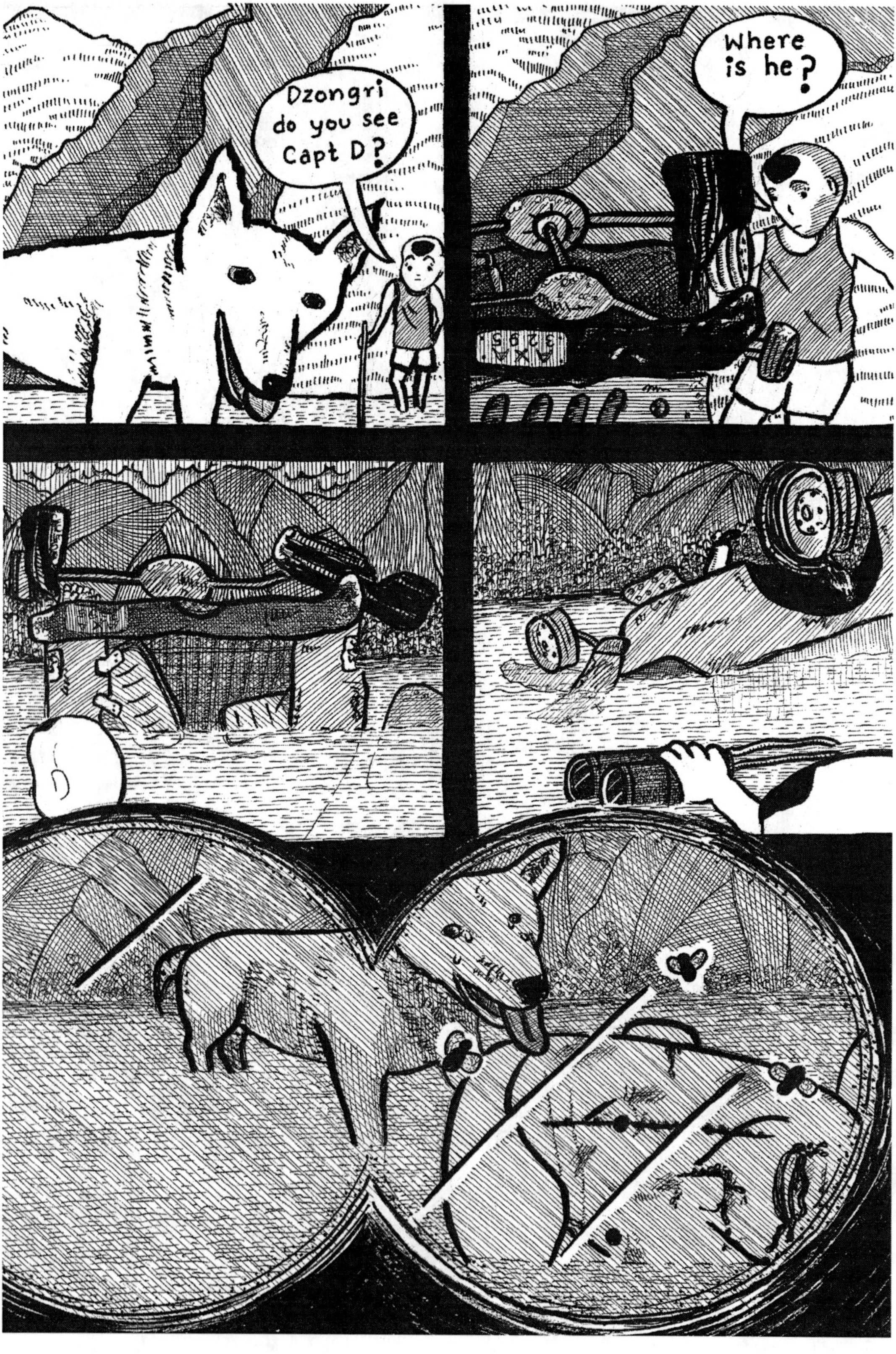
Dzongri do you see Capt D?
Where is he?

SWOOSH
ADRENALINE

Hang on Capt D!

We were meeting Captain D. You just killed Captain D.
EXAMINER : Dr P. Das (Medical)
Madam here's everything on Capt D. What's not alive can't be killed. It's a secondary identity code named Capt D.
I won't miss Capt D after all.
Well Dr. Das Job very well done.
BANG
SHELL SHOCK CLINIC
PANBAZAR GUWAHATI

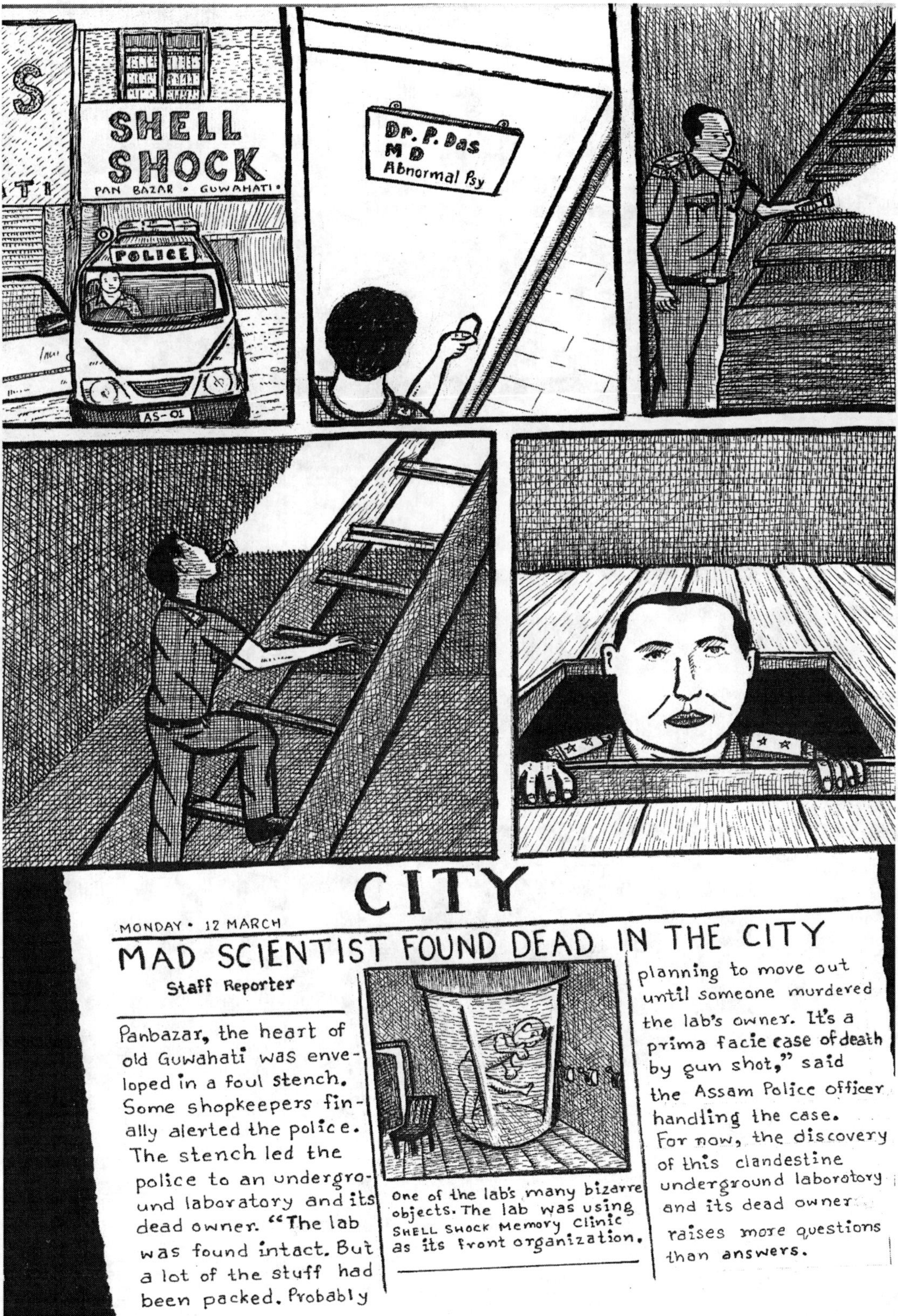
SHELL
SHOCK
PAN BAZAR • GUWAHATI •
POLICE
AS-01
Dr. P. Das
MD
Abnormal Psy
CITY
MONDAY • 12 MARCH
MAD SCIENTIST FOUND DEAD IN THE CITY
Staff Reporter
Panbazar, the heart of old Guwahati was enveloped in a foul stench. Some shopkeepers finally alerted the police. The stench led the police to an underground laboratory and its dead owner. "The lab was found intact. But a lot of the stuff had been packed. Probably planning to move out until someone murdered the lab's owner. It's a prima facie case of death by gun shot," said the Assam Police officer handling the case.
For now, the discovery of this clandestine underground laborotory and its dead owner raises more questions than answers.
One of the lab's many bizarre objects. The lab was using SHELL SHOCK Memory Clinic as its front organization.

SHELL SHOCK
PAN BAZAR • GUW ATI
TIC
TOC
ADRENALINE
"It still strikes me myself as strange that the case histories I write should read like short stories and that, as one might say, they lack the serious stamp of science. I must console myself with the reflection that the nature of the subject is evidently responsible for this, rather than any preference of my own." FREUD
TIC
TOC

11 CAPTAIN DEAD

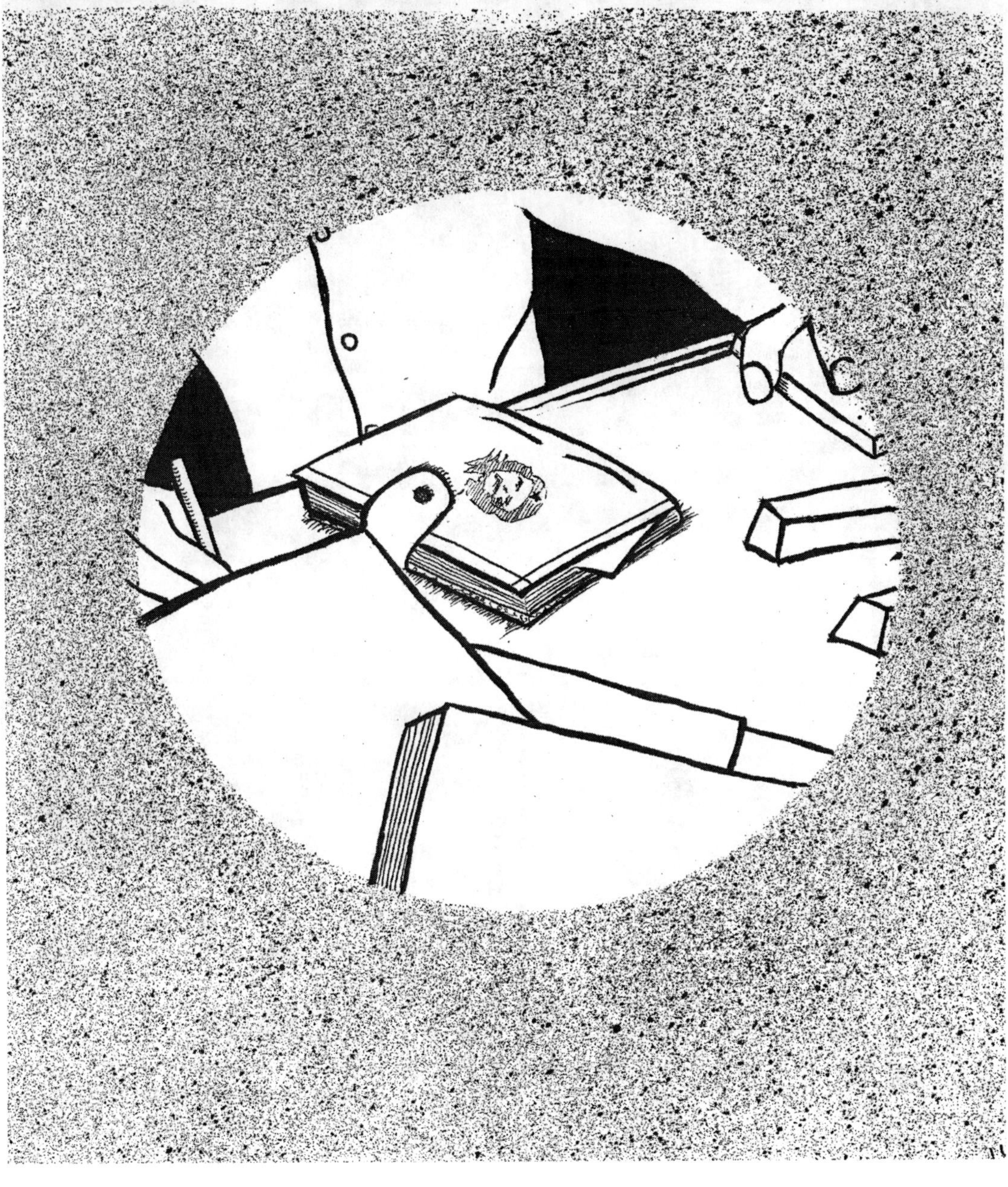

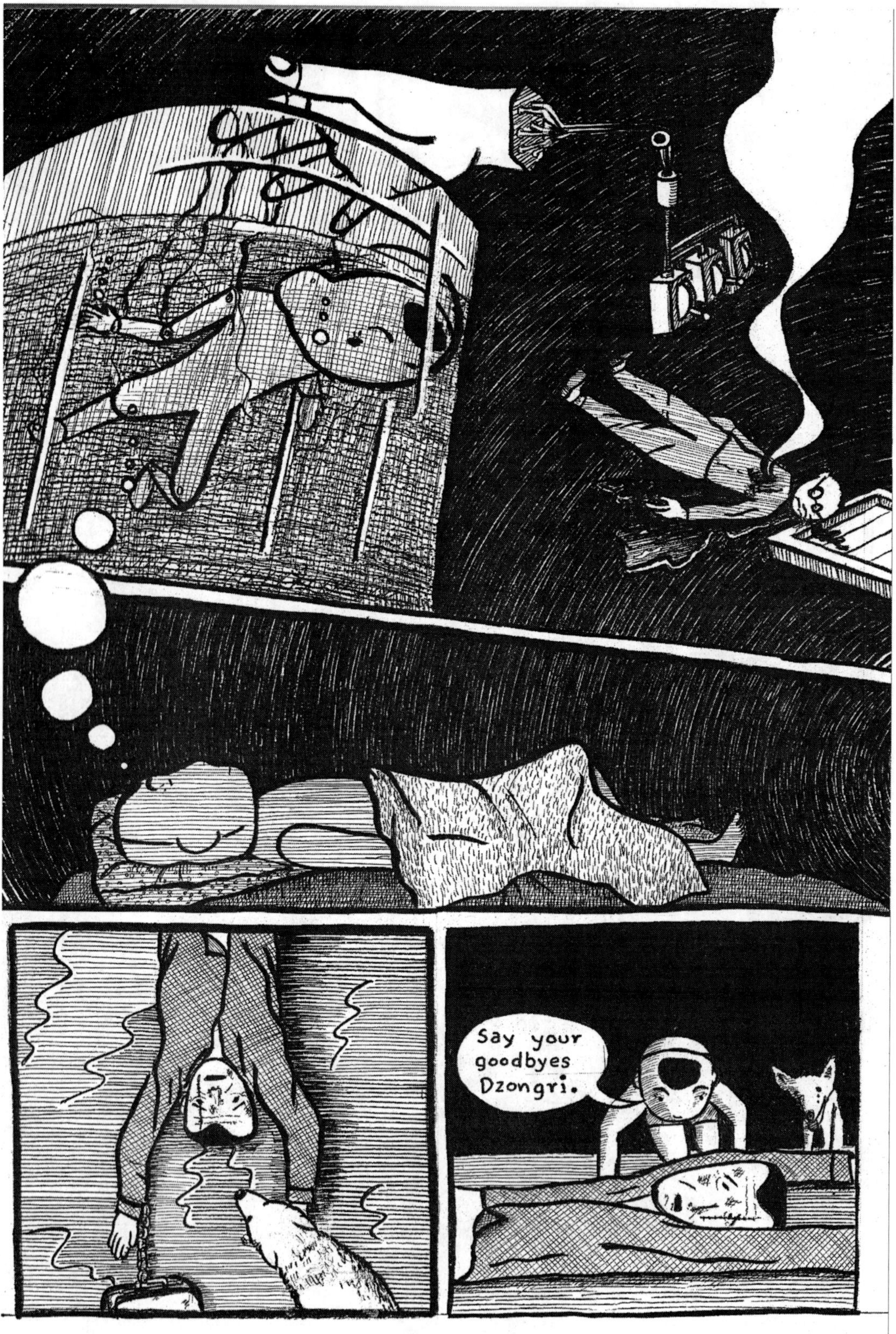
Say your goodbyes Dzongri.

BOW WOW WOW WOOF WOOF
WOOF WOOF

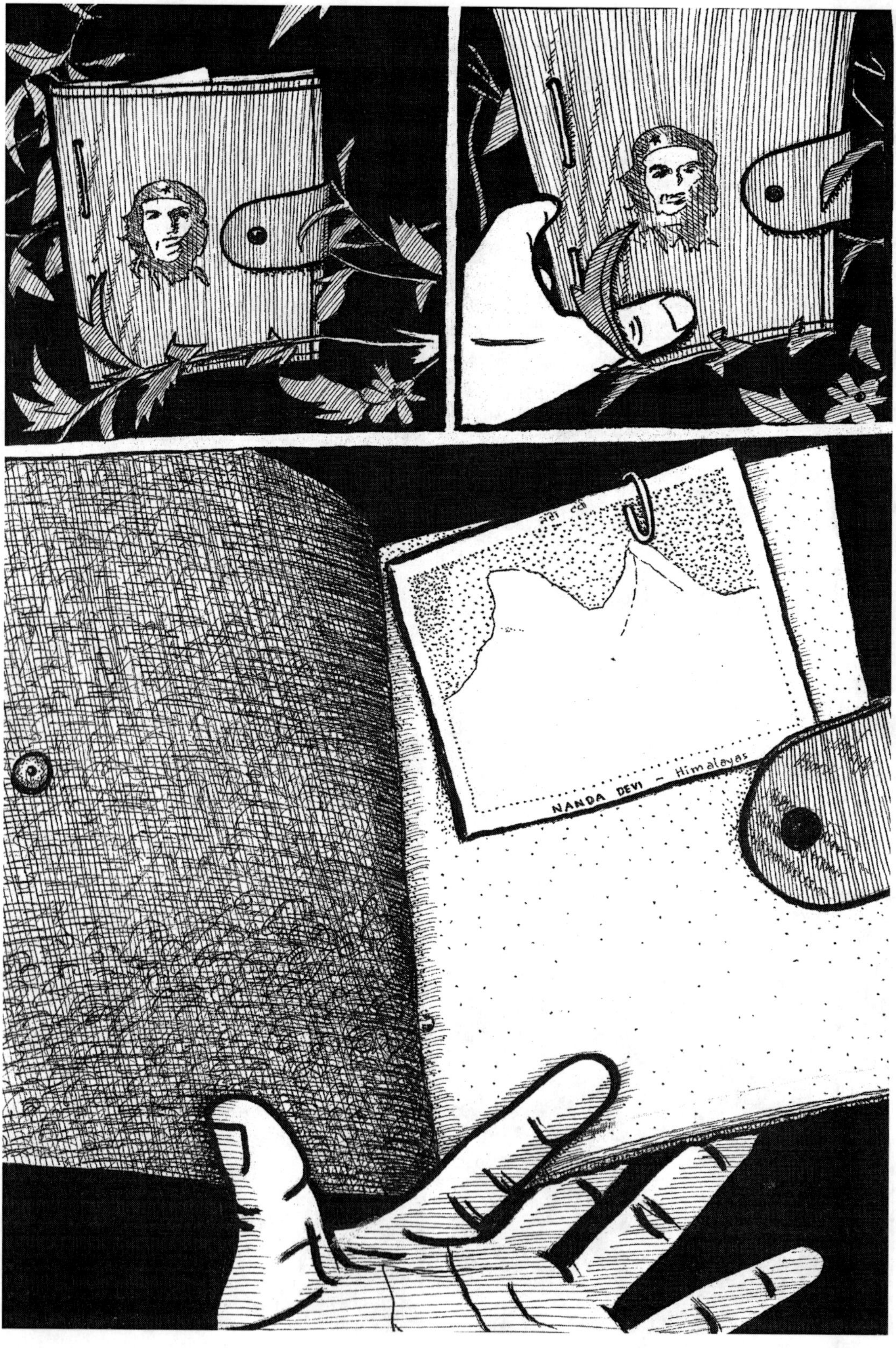
NANDA DEVI – Himalayas

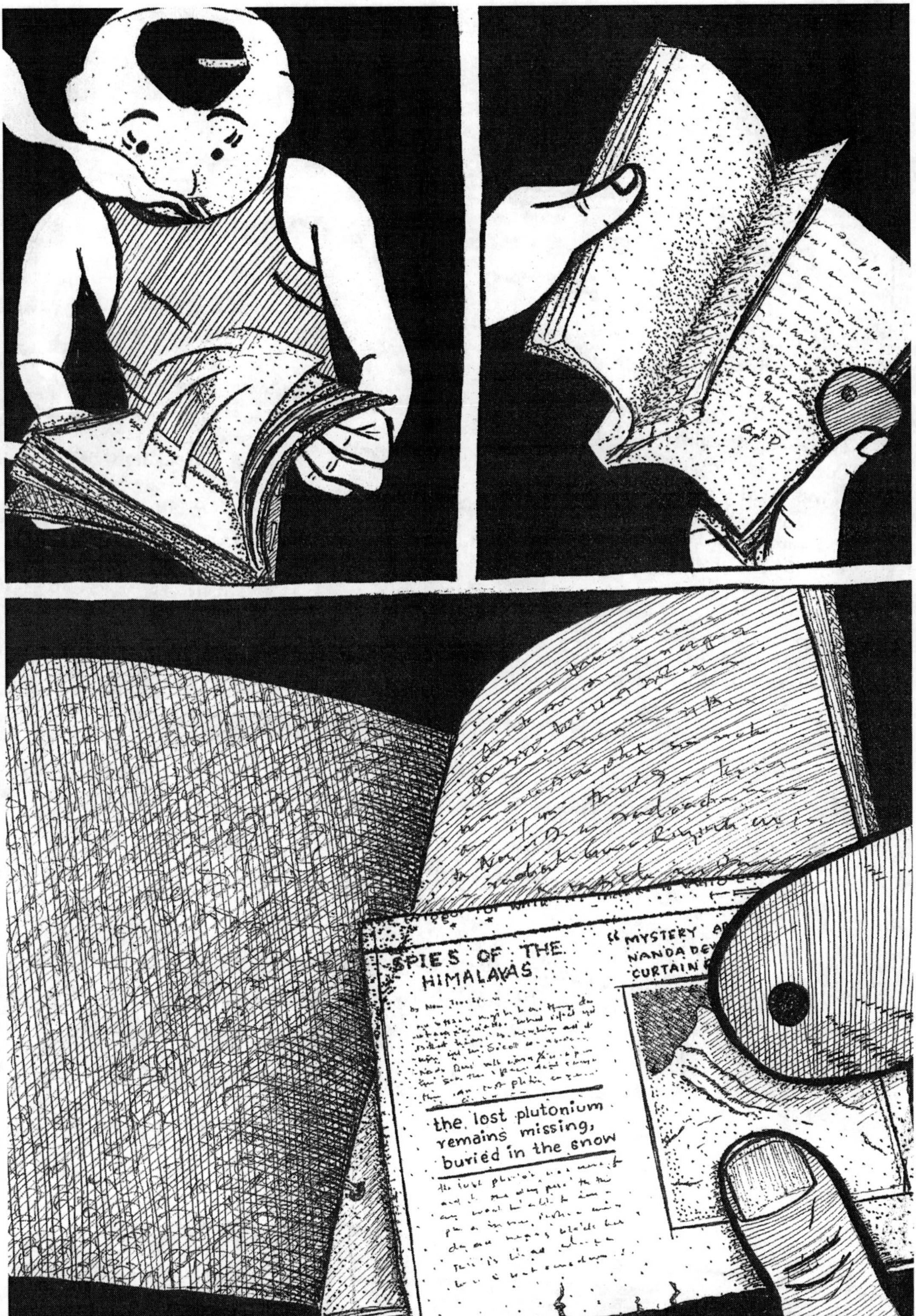
SPIES OF THE HIMALAYAS
MYSTERY
the lost plutonium remains missing, buried in the snow

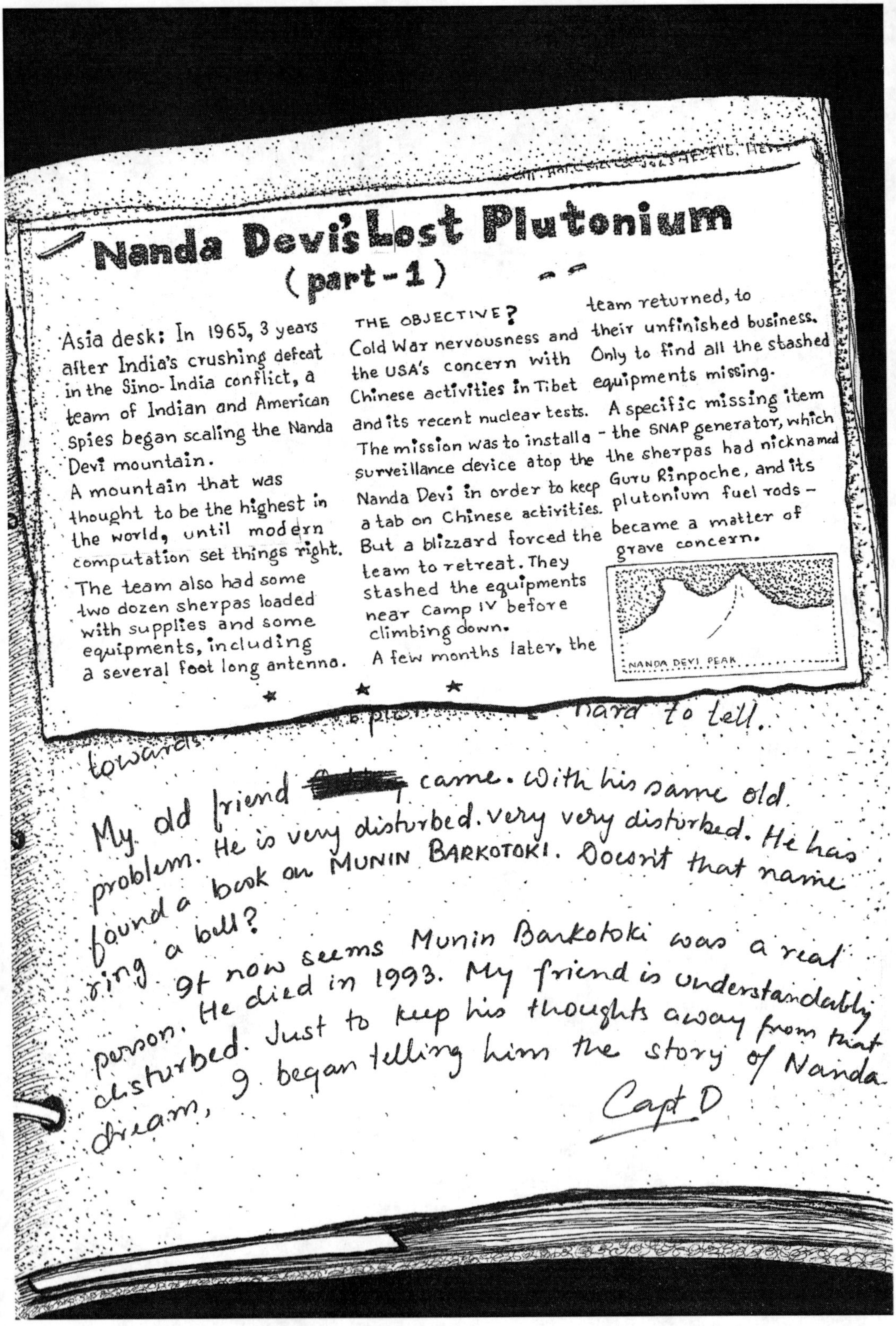
Nanda Devi's Lost Plutonium
(part-1)
Asia desk: In 1965, 3 years after India's crushing defeat in the Sino-India conflict, a team of Indian and American spies began scaling the Nanda Devi mountain.
A mountain that was thought to be the highest in the world, until modern computation set things right.
The team also had some two dozen sherpas loaded with supplies and some equipments, including a several foot long antenna.
THE OBJECTIVE?
Cold War nervousness and the USA's concern with Chinese activities in Tibet and its recent nuclear tests.
The mission was to install a surveillance device atop the Nanda Devi in order to keep a tab on Chinese activities.
But a blizzard forced the team to retreat. They stashed the equipments near Camp IV before climbing down.
A few months later, the team returned, to their unfinished business. Only to find all the stashed equipments missing.
A specific missing item - the SNAP generator, which the sherpas had nicknamed Guru Rinpoche, and its plutonium fuel rods - became a matter of grave concern.
NANDA DEVI PEAK
hard to tell.
towards
My old friend came. With his same old problem. He is very disturbed. very very disturbed. He has found a book on MUNIN BARKOTOKI. Doesn't that name ring a bell?
It now seems Munin Barkotoki was a real person. He died in 1993. My friend is understandably disturbed. Just to keep his thoughts away from that dream, I began telling him the story of Nanda
Capt D

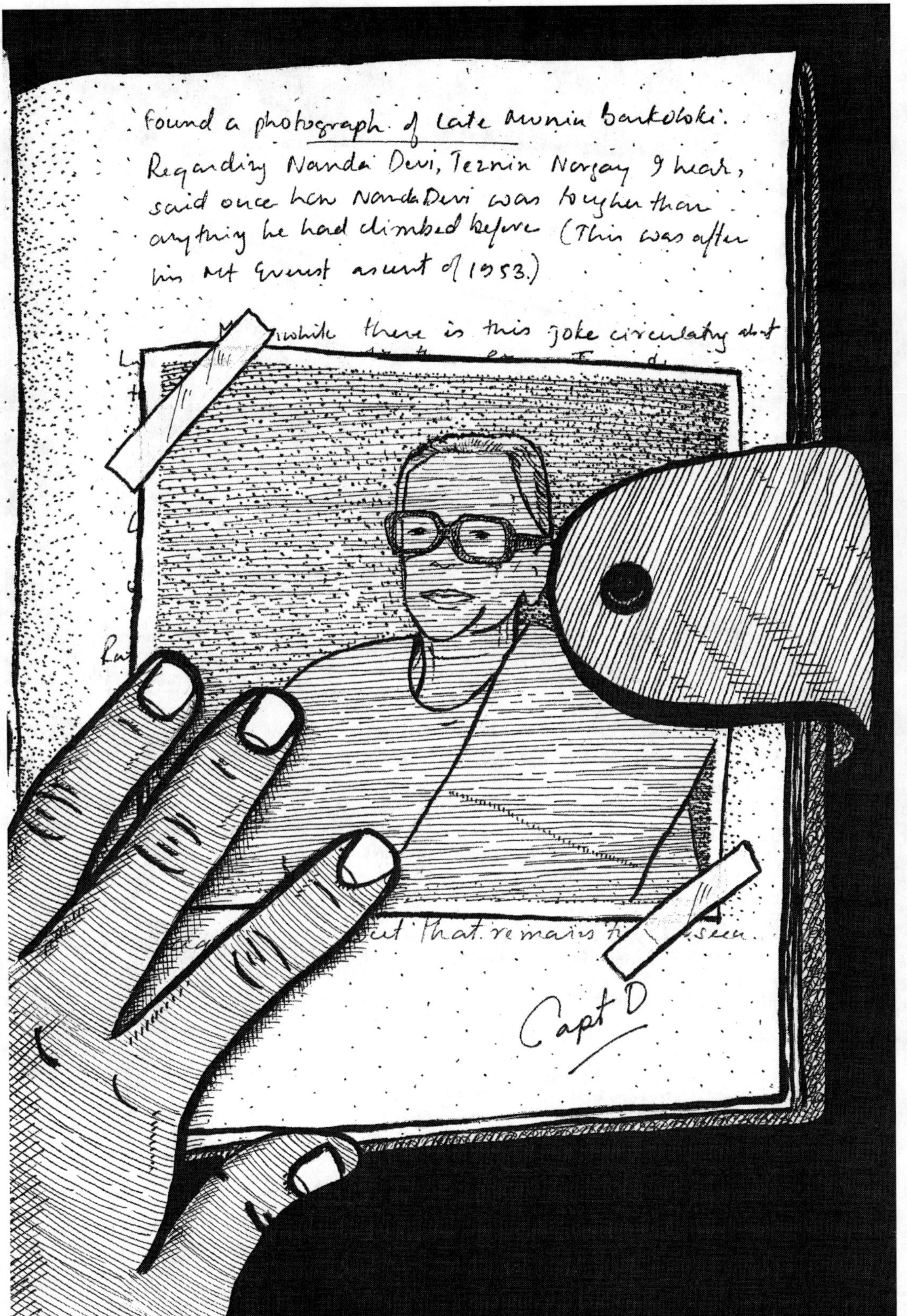
Found a photograph of late Arunin Barkoloki.
Regarding Nanda Devi, Tenzin Norgay I hear, said once how Nanda Devi was tougher than anything he had climbed before (This was after his ref Everest ascent of 1953.)
there is this joke circulating about
that remains to be seen
Capt D

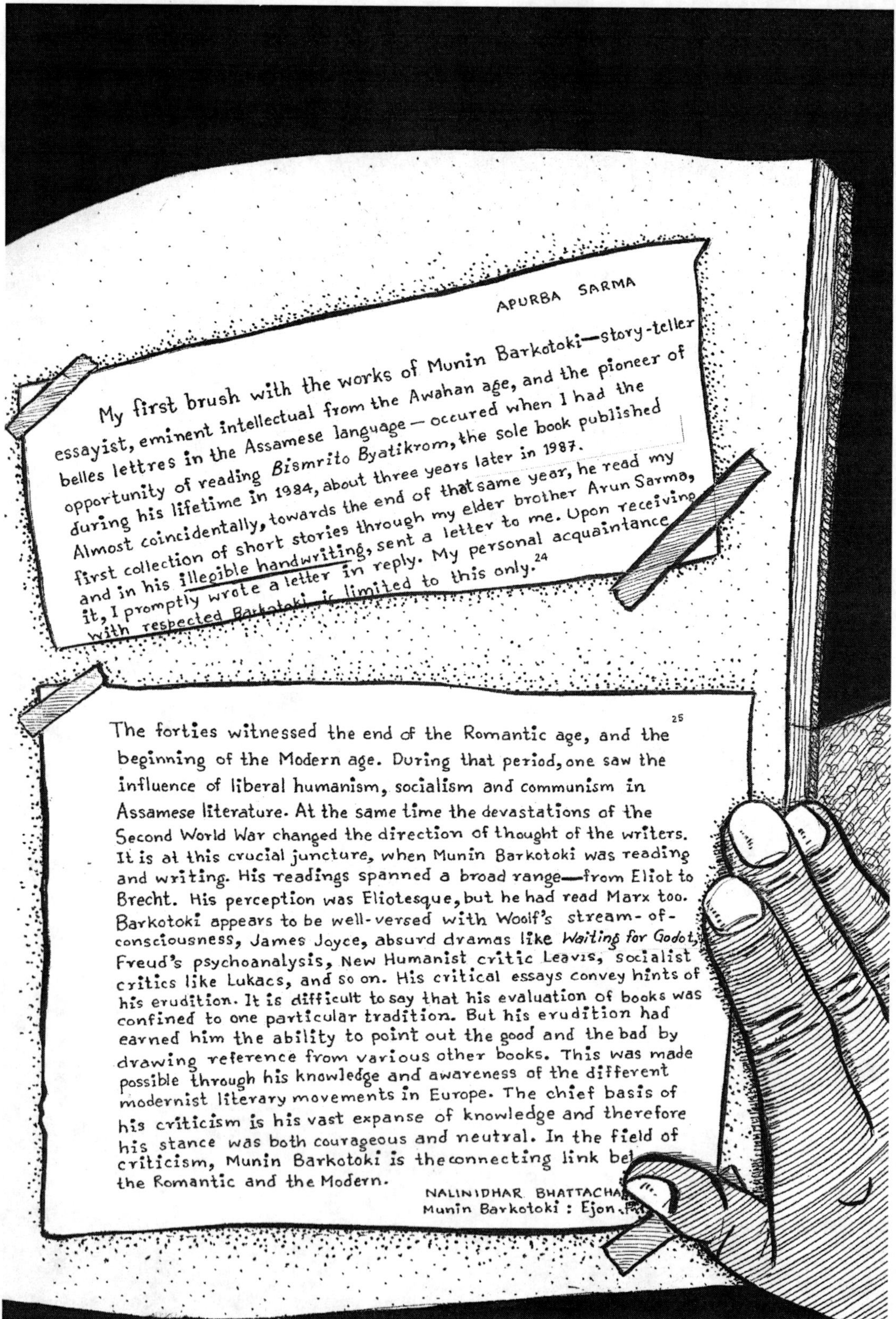
APURBA SARMA
My first brush with the works of Munin Barkotoki—story-teller essayist, eminent intellectual from the Awahan age, and the pioneer of belles lettres in the Assamese language—occured when I had the opportunity of reading Bismrito Byatikrom, the sole book published during his lifetime in 1984, about three years later in 1987. Almost coincidentally, towards the end of that same year, he read my first collection of short stories through my elder brother Arun Sarma, and in his illegible handwriting, sent a letter to me. Upon receiving it, I promptly wrote a letter in reply. My personal acquaintance with respected Barkotoki is limited to this only.[24]
The forties witnessed the end of the Romantic age, and the beginning of the Modern age. During that period, one saw the influence of liberal humanism, socialism and communism in Assamese literature. At the same time the devastations of the Second World War changed the direction of thought of the writers. It is at this crucial juncture, when Munin Barkotoki was reading and writing. His readings spanned a broad range—from Eliot to Brecht. His perception was Eliotesque, but he had read Marx too. Barkotoki appears to be well-versed with Woolf's stream-of-consciousness, James Joyce, absurd dramas like Waiting for Godot, Freud's psychoanalysis, New Humanist critic Leavis, socialist critics like Lukacs, and so on. His critical essays convey hints of his erudition. It is difficult to say that his evaluation of books was confined to one particular tradition. But his erudition had earned him the ability to point out the good and the bad by drawing reference from various other books. This was made possible through his knowledge and awareness of the different modernist literary movements in Europe. The chief basis of his criticism is his vast expanse of knowledge and therefore his stance was both courageous and neutral. In the field of criticism, Munin Barkotoki is the connecting link bet
the Romantic and the Modern.[25]
NALINIDHAR BHATTACHA
Munin Barkotoki : Ejon

BIG BERTHA
The Barkotoki diaries turned out to be an
impregnable fortress of his bad handwriting.
What may have been a ready-to-serve autobiography
The Great War began in 1914 and Barkotoki was
born in 1915. Improvement/advancement in artillery &
big guns marked the end of traditional 'FORT'
based warfare. BIG GUNS like the BIG BERTHA,
shattered forts, and that led to 'TRENCH warfare'.
I too, brought out a BIG BERTHA, to bring
down the fortress of BAD HANDWRITING. Did it help?
What's there to magnify? Only lines, dots and dashes.
Bad handwriting? It's not writing! Period.
But the night took on a weird turn. Just like my
OLD FRIEND, I went into a dream. Late Barkotoki
sniffing through his handwritten diaries, while I lay
there asleep on the table. I tried to wake myself up.
Like I said WEIRD.
Capt D.
1914. A FORT HIT BY A BIG BERTHA SHELL
BIG BERTHA

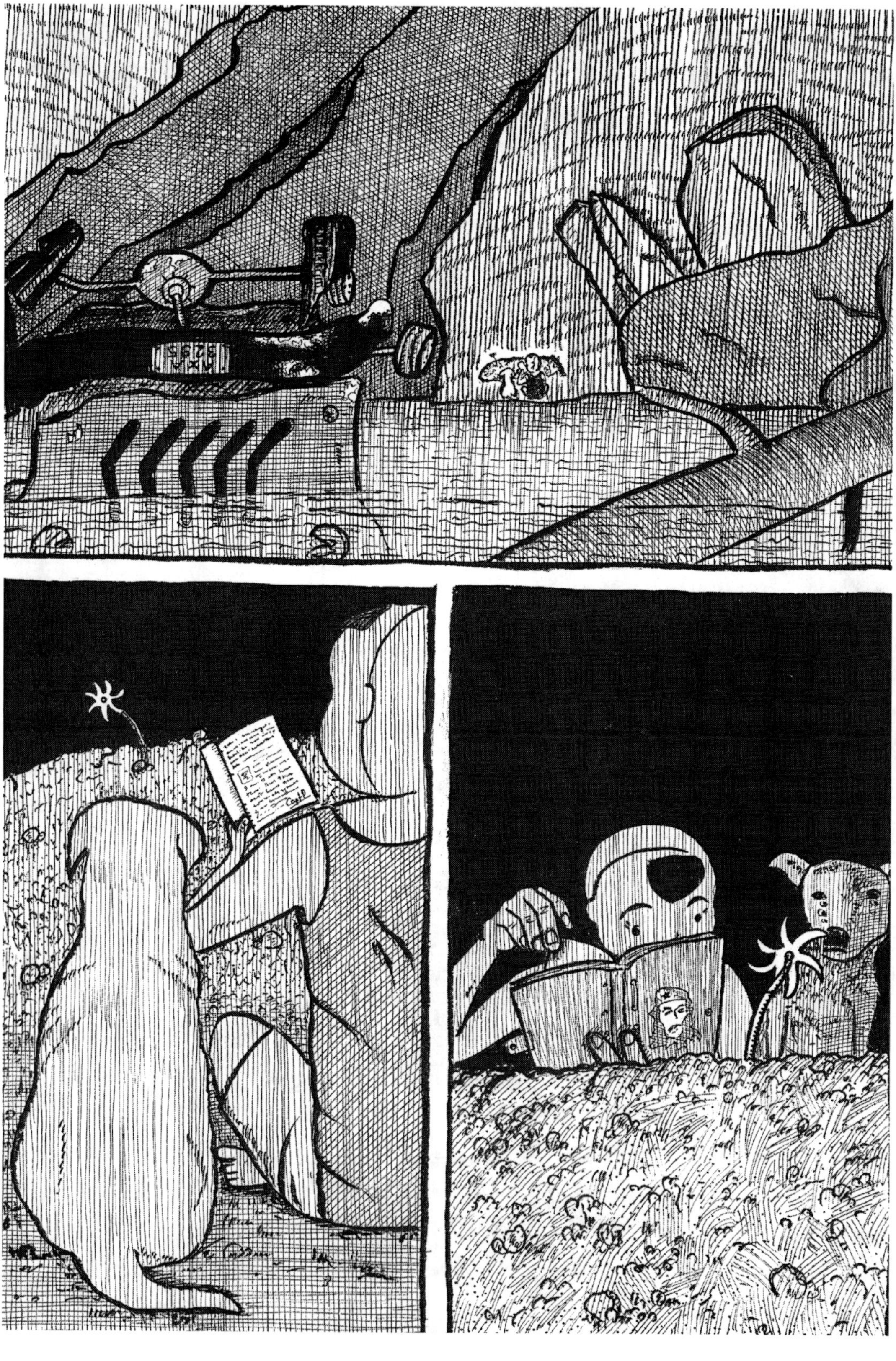

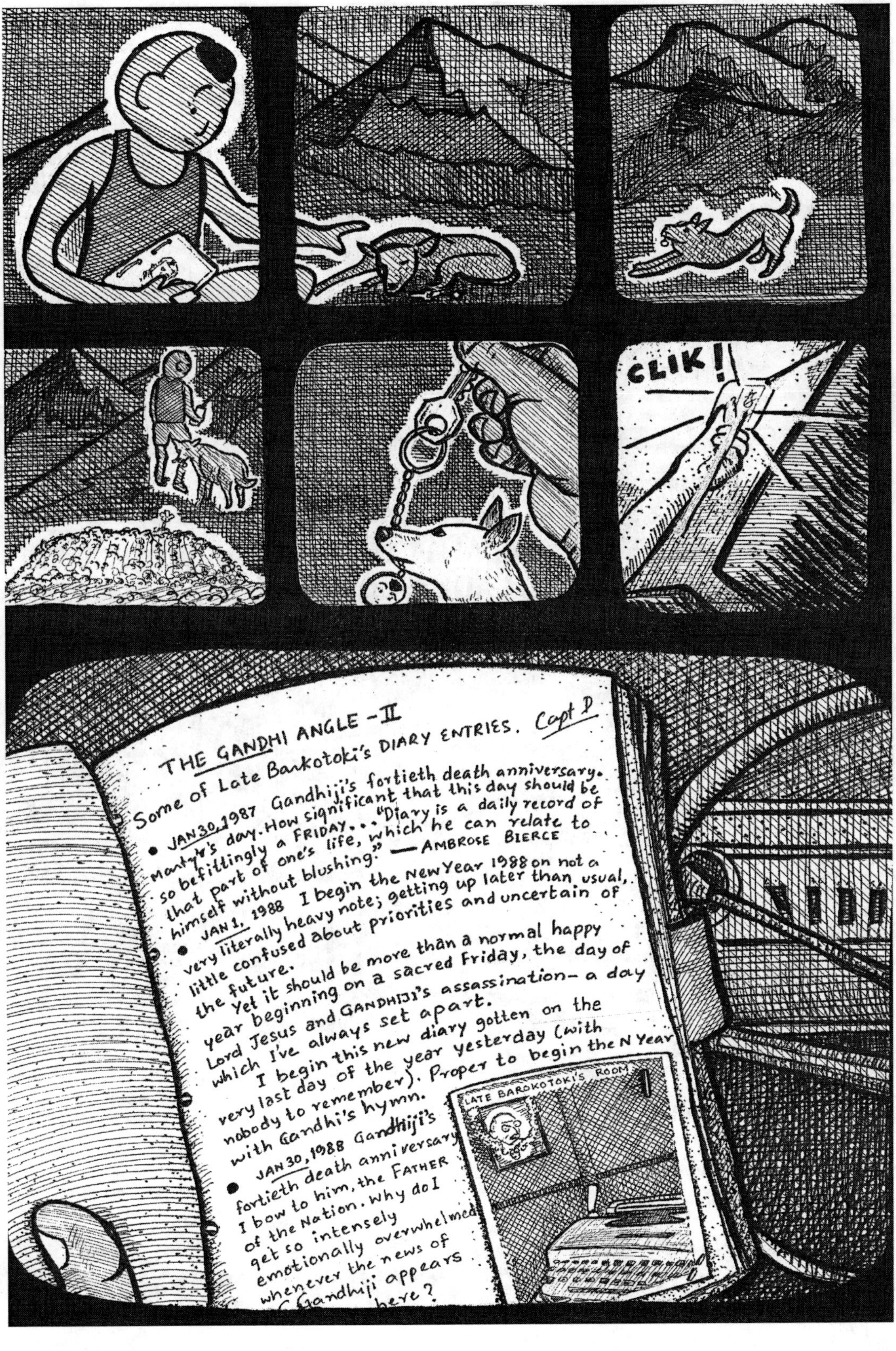
CLIK!
THE GANDHI ANGLE - II
Some of Late Barkotoki's DIARY ENTRIES. Capt D
• JAN 30, 1987 Gandhiji's fortieth death anniversary. Martyr's day. How significant that this day should be so befittingly a FRIDAY... "Diary is a daily record of that part of one's life, which he can relate to himself without blushing." — AMBROSE BIERCE
• JAN 1, 1988 I begin the New Year 1988 on not a very literally heavy note; getting up later than usual, little confused about priorities and uncertain of the future.
Yet it should be more than a normal happy year beginning on a sacred Friday, the day of Lord Jesus and GANDHIJI's assassination - a day which I've always set apart.
I begin this new diary gotten on the very last day of the year yesterday (with nobody to remember). Proper to begin the N Year with Gandhi's hymn.
• JAN 30, 1988 Gandhiji's fortieth death anniversary I bow to him, the FATHER of the Nation. Why do I get so intensely emotionally overwhelmed whenever the news of Gandhiji appears here?
LATE BAROKOTOKI'S ROOM

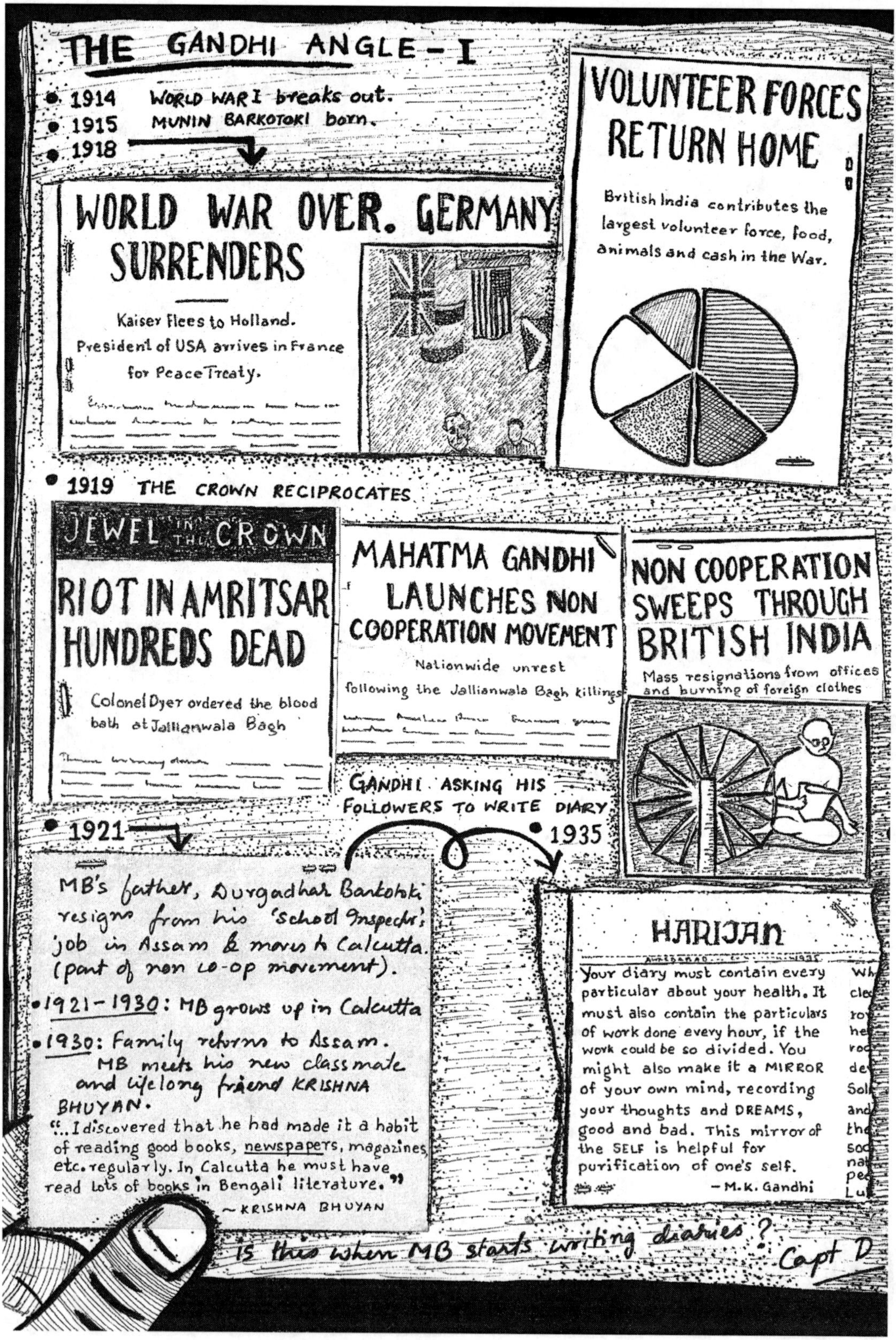

THE GANDHI ANGLE - I
• 1914 WORLD WAR I breaks out.
• 1915 MUNIN BARKOTOKI born.
• 1918
WORLD WAR OVER. GERMANY SURRENDERS
Kaiser Flees to Holland. President of USA arrives in France for Peace Treaty.
VOLUNTEER FORCES RETURN HOME
British India contributes the largest volunteer force, food, animals and cash in the War.
• 1919 THE CROWN RECIPROCATES
JEWEL IN THE CROWN
RIOT IN AMRITSAR HUNDREDS DEAD
Colonel Dyer ordered the blood bath at Jallianwala Bagh
MAHATMA GANDHI LAUNCHES NON COOPERATION MOVEMENT
Nationwide unrest following the Jallianwala Bagh killings
NON COOPERATION SWEEPS THROUGH BRITISH INDIA
Mass resignations from offices and burning of foreign clothes
GANDHI ASKING HIS FOLLOWERS TO WRITE DIARY
• 1921
• 1935
MB's father, Durgadhar Barkotoki resigns from his 'School Inspector's' job in Assam & moves to Calcutta. (part of non co-op movement).
• 1921–1930: MB grows up in Calcutta
• 1930: Family returns to Assam. MB meets his new classmate and lifelong friend KRISHNA BHUYAN.
"...I discovered that he had made it a habit of reading good books, newspapers, magazines, etc. regularly. In Calcutta he must have read lots of books in Bengali literature."
~ KRISHNA BHUYAN
HARIJAN
Your diary must contain every particular about your health. It must also contain the particulars of work done every hour, if the work could be so divided. You might also make it a MIRROR of your own mind, recording your thoughts and DREAMS, good and bad. This mirror of the SELF is helpful for purification of one's self.
– M.K. Gandhi
Is this when MB starts writing diaries?
Capt D

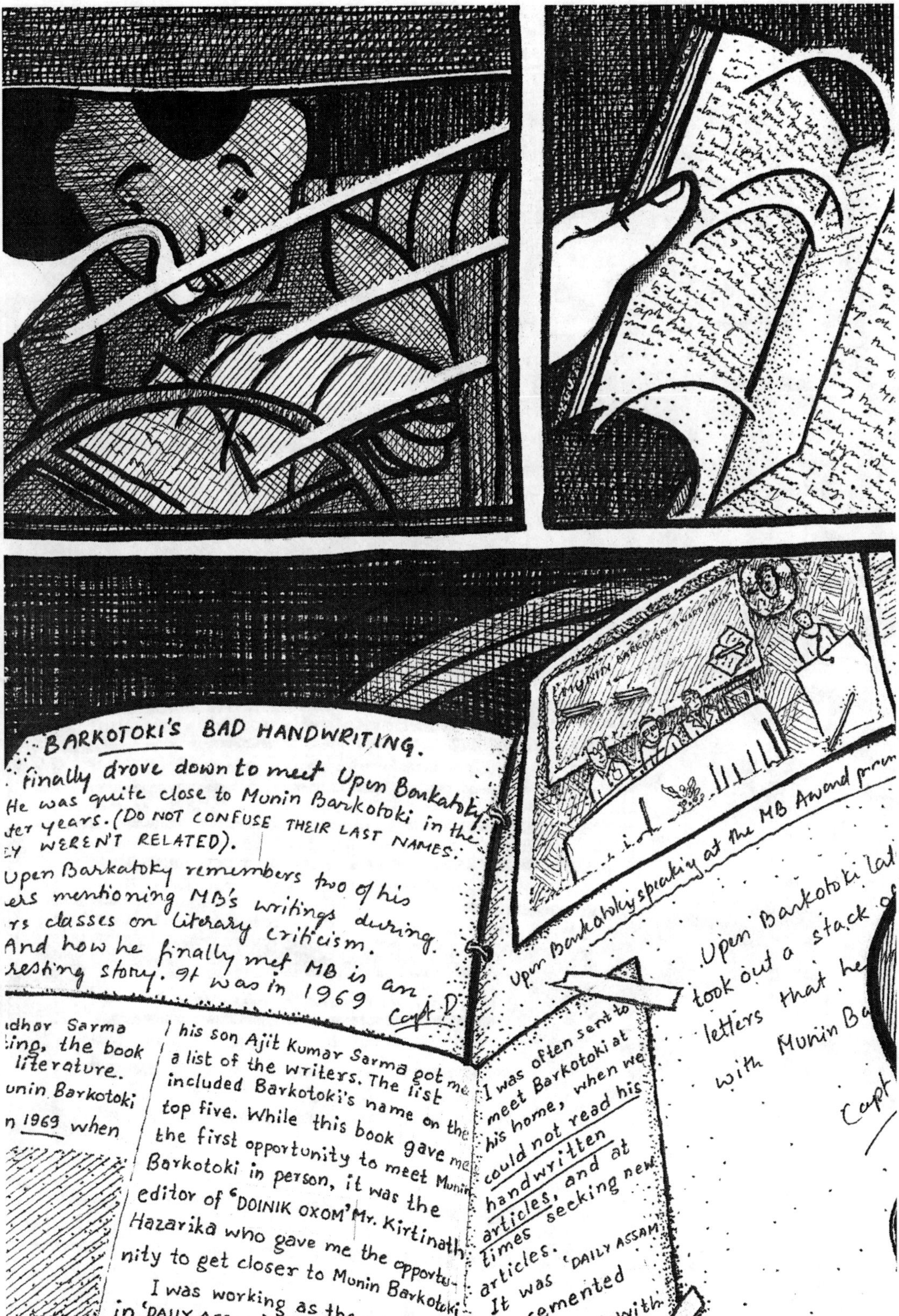
BARKOTOKI'S BAD HANDWRITING.
finally drove down to meet Upen Barkatoky
He was quite close to Munin Barkotoki in the
ter years. (DO NOT CONFUSE THEIR LAST NAMES.
Y WEREN'T RELATED).
Upen Barkatoky remembers two of his
ers mentioning MB's writings during
rs classes on literary criticism.
And how he finally met MB is an
resting story. It was in 1969
Capt D.
MUNIN BARKOTOKI AWARD
Upen Barkatoky speaking at the MB Award pre
Upen Barkotoki lat
took out a stack o
letters that he
with Munin Ba
Capt
dhar Sarma
ting, the book
literature.
unin Barkotoki
n 1969 when
his son Ajit Kumar Sarma got me
a list of the writers. The list
included Barkotoki's name on the
top five. While this book gave me
the first opportunity to meet Munin
Barkotoki in person, it was the
editor of 'DOINIK OXOM' Mr. Kirtinath
Hazarika who gave me the opportu-
nity to get closer to Munin Barkotoki
I was working as the sub
in 'DAILY ASSAM'
I was often sent to
meet Barkotoki at
his home, when we
could not read his
handwritten
articles, and at
times seeking new
articles.
It was 'DAILY ASSAM
cemented
tion with

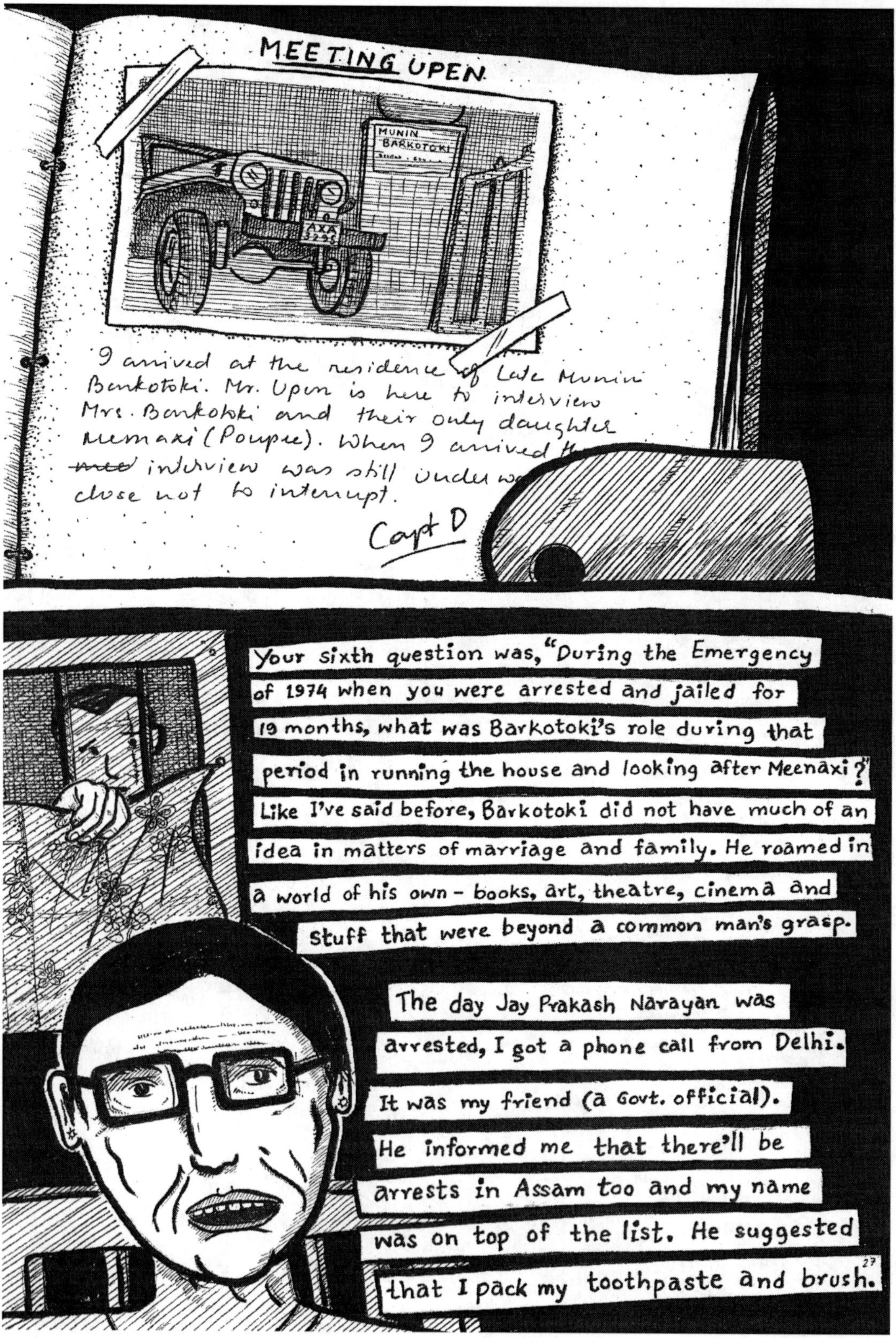
MEETING UPEN
MUNIN BARKOTOKI
AXA 3295
I arrived at the residence of Late Munin Barkotoki. Mr. Upen is here to interview Mrs. Barkotoki and their only daughter Meenaxi (Poupee). When I arrived th interview was still underw close not to interrupt.
Capt D
Your sixth question was, "During the Emergency of 1974 when you were arrested and jailed for 19 months, what was Barkotoki's role during that period in running the house and looking after Meenaxi?"
Like I've said before, Barkotoki did not have much of an idea in matters of marriage and family. He roamed in a world of his own - books, art, theatre, cinema and stuff that were beyond a common man's grasp.
The day Jay Prakash Narayan was arrested, I got a phone call from Delhi.
It was my friend (a Govt. official).
He informed me that there'll be arrests in Assam too and my name was on top of the list. He suggested that I pack my toothpaste and brush.

I couldn't figure out how Barkotoki was going to REACT to the NEWS. At around 6 in the evening an officer (won't tell his name) arrived with two policemen. Barkotoki was still not home(he went to the library every evening).
Madam you have to come to the STATION. We've got to discuss something.
Not to the station. But to the jail. I know. Have tea. Meanwhile I'll feed my daughter.
Saying so, I sent the housemaid to find Barkotoki
DISTRICT LIBRARY
SIR!
SIR!
HELP!
Sir you are the only one. I'm closing.
What else have you got? Cook? Cook late or eat out. I'll pay.
I've to read this today. It won't be here, tomorrow.
Take it Sir. Take it. You'll be here tomorrow. Bring it then.

Barkotoki finally made it home by 8. I'd meanwhile spoken to Meenaxi about the Emergency, the nationwide arrests, and why we were protesting against Indira Gandhi's leadership... just to mentally prepare her. When Barkotoki reached home, he saw policemen sipping tea. He came inside...
What happened?
They are taking Ma to the JAIL!
Ofcourse they will! The way your mom has been up against the government, outside and inside the Secretariat. Ofcourse they will.
The New York Times
It seemed Barkotoki took the news light-heartedly. I felt better. 'Come let's have food', I said and we sat for dinner.
I explained how the house was going to run in my absence and how to pay Meenaxi's school fee.
A friend will arrange for the weekly ration. Fish, vegetables and eggs
During the entire 19 months of my imprisonment, Meenaxi and Xarala ran the house, attended to guests and looked after Barkotoki
Oh everything is sorted! Meenaxi and Xarala can run the house. If anything, they can visit you in jail and ask.

12 TUNNEL of WORDS

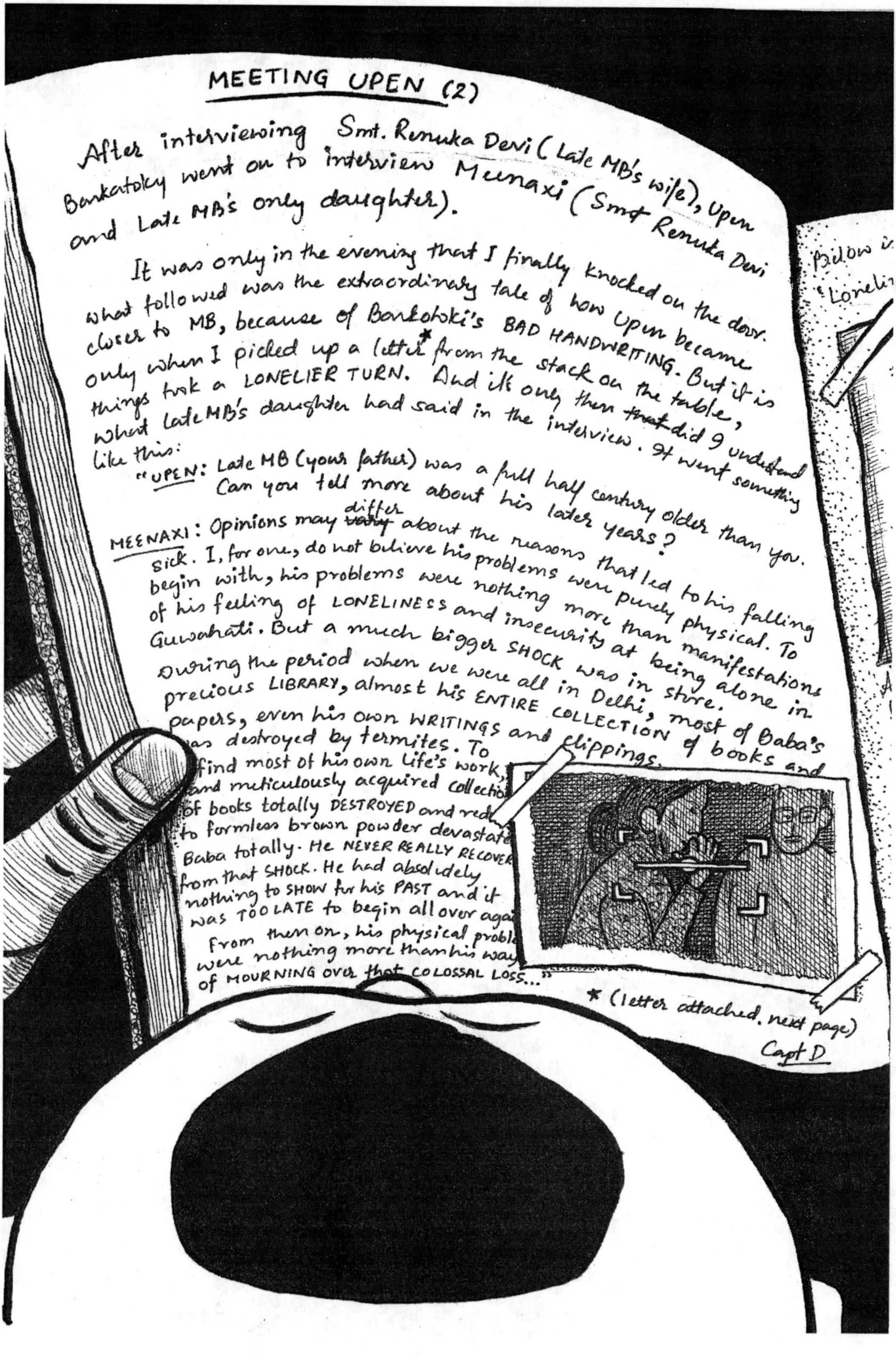
MEETING UPEN (2)
After interviewing Smt. Renuka Devi (Late MB's wife), Upen Bonkotoky went on to interview Meenaxi (Smt Renuka Devi and Late MB's only daughter).
It was only in the evening that I finally knocked on the door. What followed was the extraordinary tale of how Upen became closer to MB, because of Bonkotoki's BAD HANDWRITING. But it is only when I picked up a letter* from the stack on the table, things took a LONELIER TURN. And it's only then ~~that~~ did I understand what Late MB's daughter had said in the interview. It went something like this:
"UPEN: Late MB (your father) was a full half century older than you. Can you tell more about his later years?
MEENAXI: Opinions may ~~vary~~ differ about the reasons that led to his falling sick. I, for one, do not believe his problems were purely physical. To begin with, his problems were nothing more than manifestations of his feeling of LONELINESS and insecurity at being alone in Guwahati. But a much bigger SHOCK was in store. During the period when we were all in Delhi, most of Baba's precious LIBRARY, almost his ENTIRE COLLECTION of books and papers, even his own WRITINGS and clippings, was destroyed by termites. To find most of his own life's work, and meticulously acquired collectio
of books totally DESTROYED and red
to formless brown powder devastate
Baba totally. He NEVER REALLY RECOVER
from that SHOCK. He had absolutely nothing to SHOW for his PAST and it was TOO LATE to begin all over aga
From then on, his physical proble
were nothing more than his way of MOURNING over that COLOSSAL LOSS..."
* (letter attached. next page)
Capt D

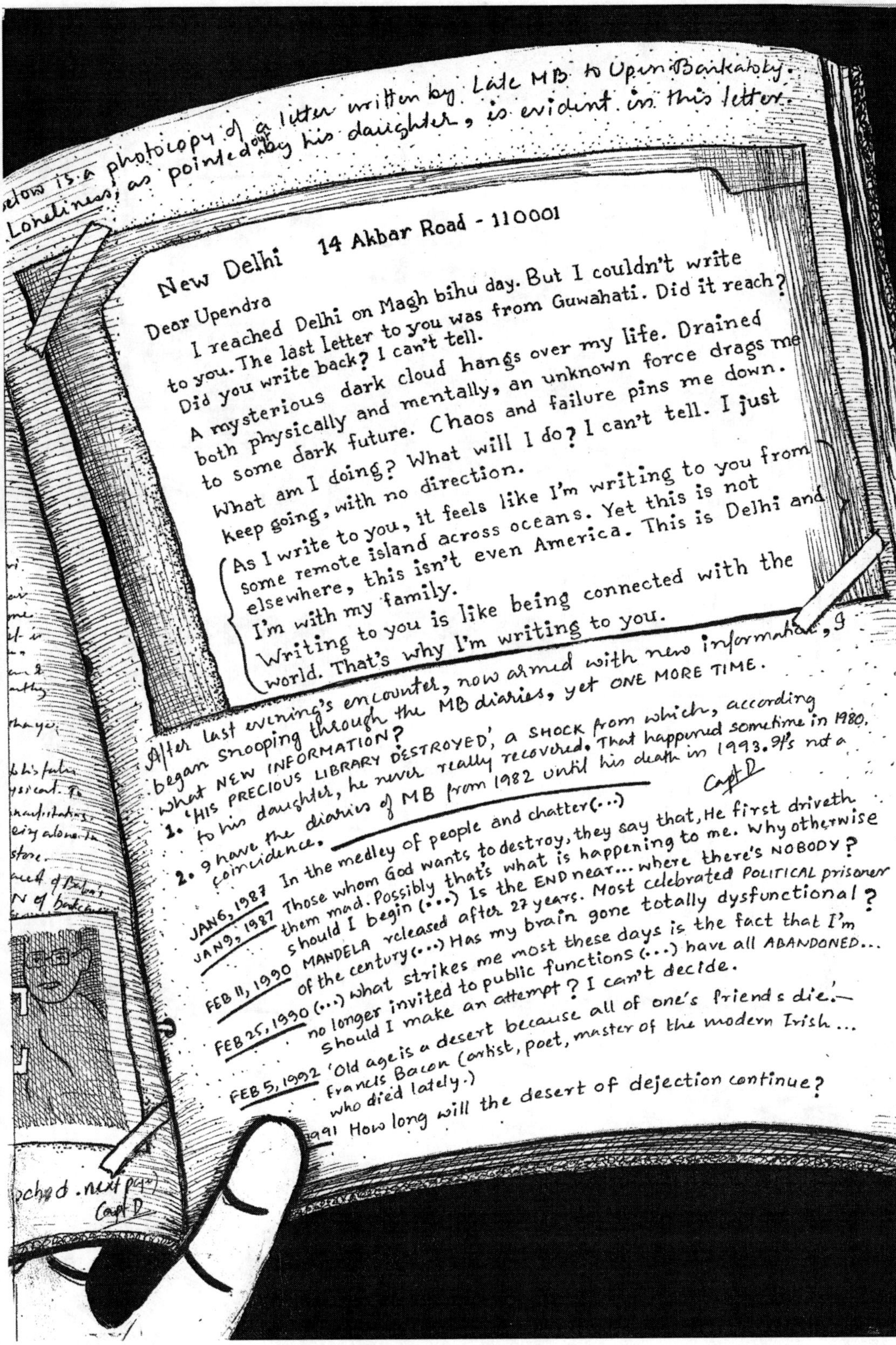

Below is a photocopy of a letter written by Late MB to Upen Barkatoky.
Loneliness, as pointed out by his daughter, is evident in this letter.
New Delhi 14 Akbar Road - 110001
Dear Upendra
I reached Delhi on Magh bihu day. But I couldn't write to you. The last letter to you was from Guwahati. Did it reach? Did you write back? I can't tell.
A mysterious dark cloud hangs over my life. Drained both physically and mentally, an unknown force drags me to some dark future. Chaos and failure pins me down.
What am I doing? What will I do? I can't tell. I just keep going, with no direction.
As I write to you, it feels like I'm writing to you from some remote island across oceans. Yet this is not elsewhere, this isn't even America. This is Delhi and I'm with my family.
Writing to you is like being connected with the world. That's why I'm writing to you.
After last evening's encounter, now armed with new information, I began snooping through the MB diaries, yet ONE MORE TIME.
What NEW INFORMATION?
1. 'HIS PRECIOUS LIBRARY DESTROYED', a SHOCK from which, according to his daughter, he never really recovered. That happened sometime in 1980.
2. I have the diaries of MB from 1982 until his death in 1993. It's not a coincidence.
Capt D
JAN 6, 1987 In the medley of people and chatter (...)
JAN 9, 1987 Those whom God wants to destroy, they say that, He first driveth them mad. Possibly that's what is happening to me. Why otherwise should I begin (...) Is the END near... where there's NOBODY?
FEB 11, 1990 MANDELA released after 27 years. Most celebrated POLITICAL prisoner of the century (...) Has my brain gone totally dysfunctional?
FEB 25, 1990 (...) What strikes me most these days is the fact that I'm no longer invited to public functions (...) have all ABANDONED... Should I make an attempt? I can't decide.
FEB 5, 1992 'Old age is a desert because all of one's friends die.' — Francis Bacon (artist, poet, master of the modern Irish ... who died lately.)
1991 How long will the desert of dejection continue?
Capt D

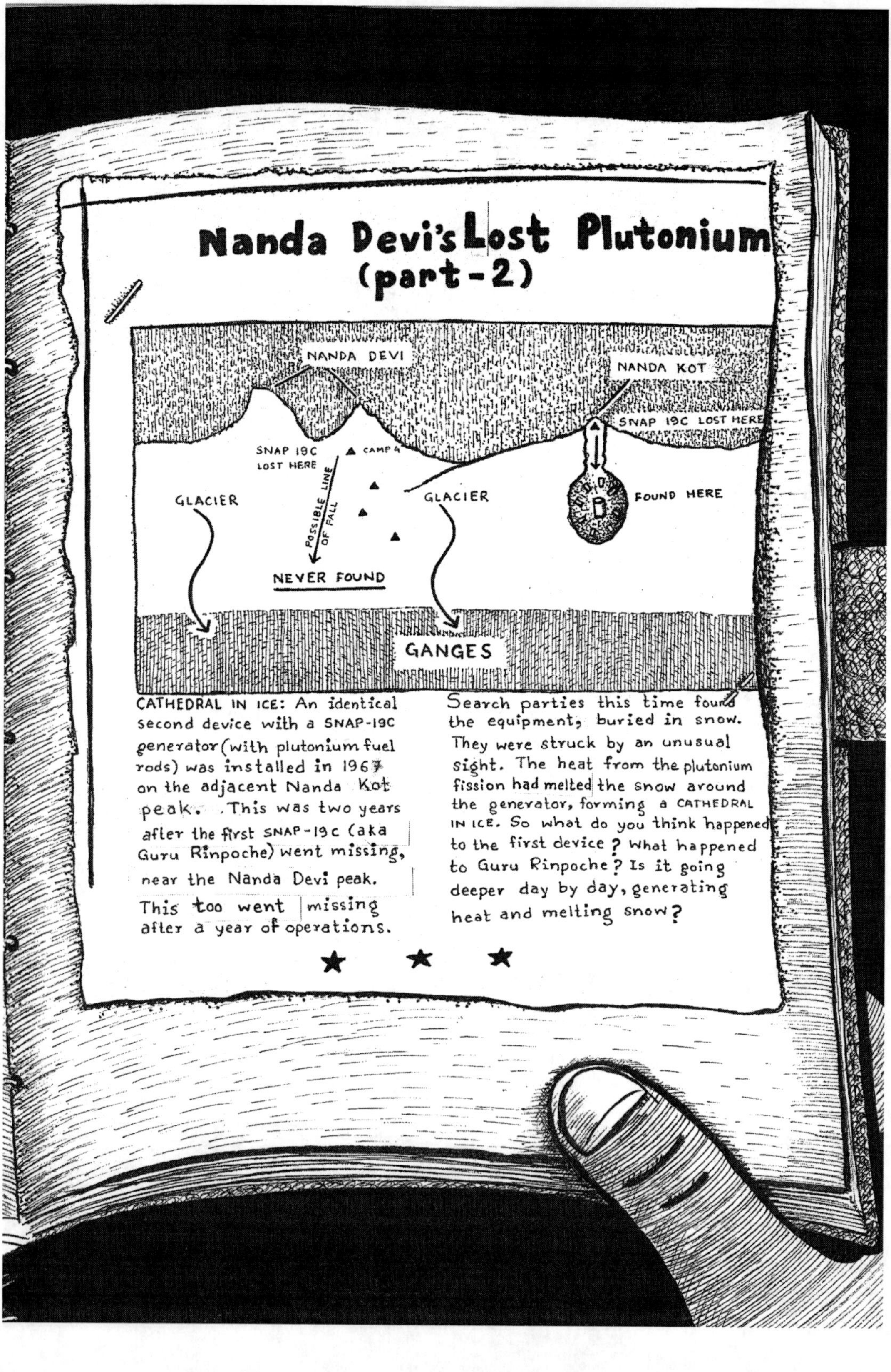
Nanda Devi's Lost Plutonium
(part-2)
NANDA DEVI
NANDA KOT
SNAP 19C LOST HERE
SNAP 19C
LOST HERE
CAMP 4
POSSIBLE LINE
OF FALL
GLACIER
GLACIER
FOUND HERE
NEVER FOUND
GANGES
CATHEDRAL IN ICE: An identical second device with a SNAP-19C generator (with plutonium fuel rods) was installed in 1967 on the adjacent Nanda Kot peak. This was two years after the first SNAP-19C (aka Guru Rinpoche) went missing, near the Nanda Devi peak. This too went missing after a year of operations.
Search parties this time found the equipment, buried in snow. They were struck by an unusual sight. The heat from the plutonium fission had melted the snow around the generator, forming a CATHEDRAL IN ICE. So what do you think happened to the first device? What happened to Guru Rinpoche? Is it going deeper day by day, generating heat and melting snow?
★ ★ ★

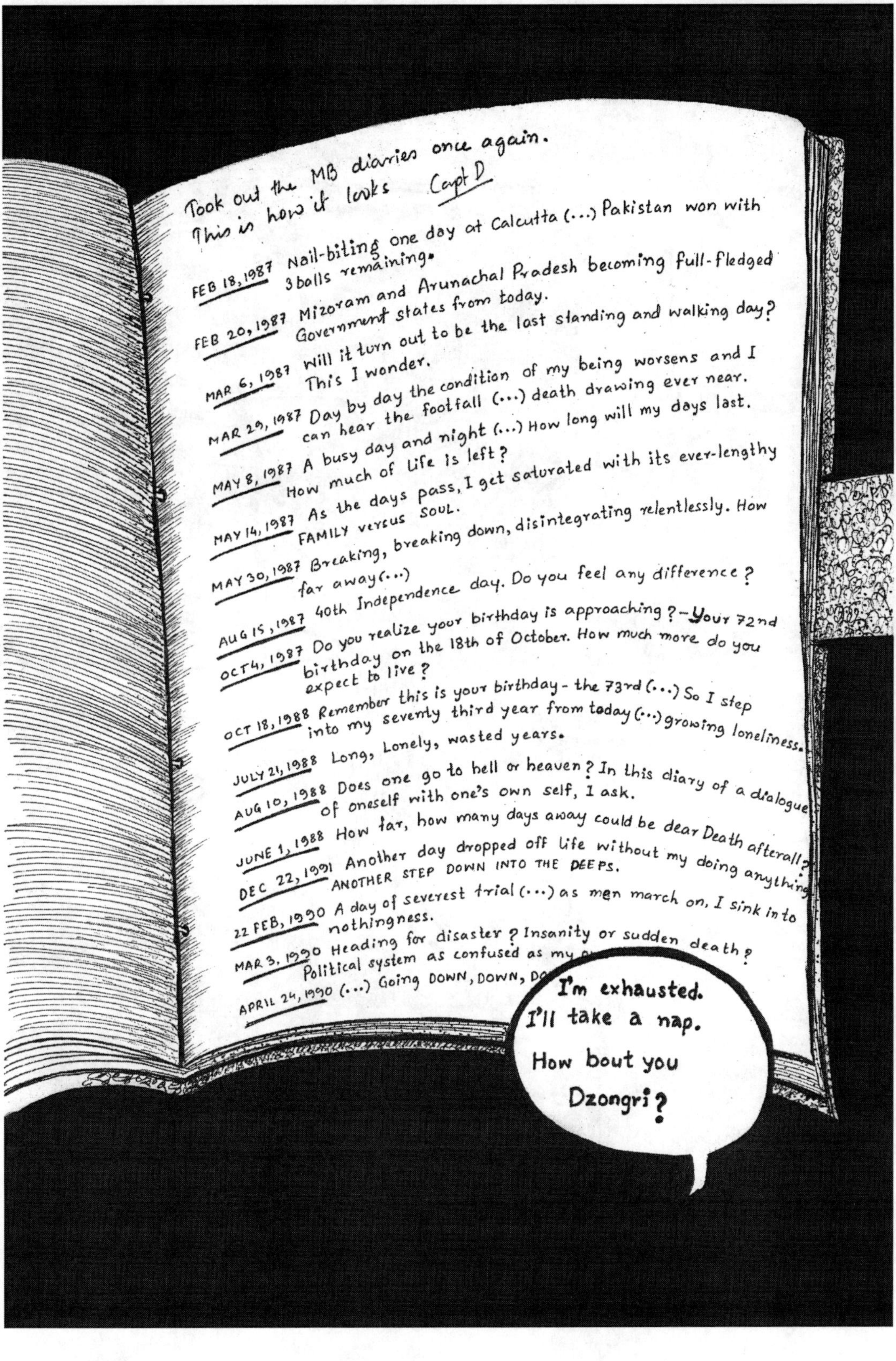
Took out the MB diaries once again.
This is how it looks Capt D
FEB 18, 1987 Nail-biting one day at Calcutta (...) Pakistan won with 3 balls remaining.
FEB 20, 1987 Mizoram and Arunachal Pradesh becoming full-fledged Government states from today.
MAR 6, 1987 Will it turn out to be the last standing and walking day? This I wonder.
MAR 29, 1987 Day by day the condition of my being worsens and I can hear the footfall (...) death drawing ever near.
MAY 8, 1987 A busy day and night (...) How long will my days last. How much of life is left?
MAY 14, 1987 As the days pass, I get saturated with its ever-lengthy FAMILY versus SOUL.
MAY 30, 1987 Breaking, breaking down, disintegrating relentlessly. How far away (...)
AUG 15, 1987 40th Independence day. Do you feel any difference?
OCT 4, 1987 Do you realize your birthday is approaching? - Your 72nd birthday on the 18th of October. How much more do you expect to live?
OCT 18, 1988 Remember this is your birthday - the 73rd (...) So I step into my seventy third year from today (...) growing loneliness.
JULY 21, 1988 Long, Lonely, wasted years.
AUG 10, 1988 Does one go to hell or heaven? In this diary of a dialogue of oneself with one's own self, I ask.
JUNE 1, 1988 How far, how many days away could be dear Death afterall?
DEC 22, 1991 Another day dropped off life without my doing anything. ANOTHER STEP DOWN INTO THE DEEPS.
22 FEB, 1990 A day of severest trial (...) as men march on, I sink into nothingness.
MAR 3, 1990 Heading for disaster? Insanity or sudden death? Political system as confused as my
APRIL 24, 1990 (...) Going DOWN, DOWN,
I'm exhausted. I'll take a nap. How bout you Dzongri?

1990
June
25
descending down the spiral... there is death to wait for.
only death
GANDHI
UNGODLY INTERVIEW WITH

EPILOGUE
...
Very well. Alright!
Capt D, do you remember anything... about how you first came here?
WE ARRIVED HERE IN 1962. LIKE I'VE BEEN TELLING DOCTOR DAS. WE'D BEEN MARCHING ON FOOT FOR SEVEN DAYS. WE WERE WET, HUNGRY AND EXHAUSTED. BUT TEZPUR TURNED OUT TO BE A GHOST TOWN.
Ghost town! You must've met Someone!
TEZPUR MENTAL HOSPITAL ESTD 1876
A WILD BUNCH. THEY WERE NUTS! MUST BE ESCAPEES FROM THE MENTAL HOSPITAL. WHAT AN AMUSING BUNCH!
They were set free, fearing a Chines invasion.
So did you make an attempt to interact?
THEY WERE PREOCCUPIED WITH SOME BIZARRE GAME OF TUG OF WAR, WITHOUT A ROPE. BUT WE DECIDED TO CAMP INSIDE IT.

COVER ALL WINDOWS! USE ANYTHING THAT YOU CAN FIND.
THE NEXT MOMENT-A BRIGHT FLASH OF LIGHT AND A DEAFENING EXPLOSION...
NEXT THING I KNOW IS THIS ROOM.
...HOW ARE YOU PASSING YOUR DAYS HERE?
ON GROUNDS OF GOOD BEHAVIOUR, I'M ALLOWED TO THE LIBRARY
AWAHAN
Awahan, Vol VII, No12
Confessions
Munin Barkotoki
Dear Editor,
The very address, 'Dear Editor,' must have led you to instantly conclude that this is nothing but a brief from the writer
TIME FOR YOU TO GET SOME SLEEP.
Let's have a look at your file. Unm... examined by Dr P. Das...
PATIENT RECORD
Patient Name / No
Capt D / 3295
Examined by
Dr. P. Das
Date
18.11.62
1. No Physical injury (SHELL SHOCKED)
2. Dissociative Identity Disord (SPLIT)
3. Functional neurosis (canno

MUNIN
BARKOTOKI

Poupee, get the 'lettera'.
Thank you!
CONFESSIONS*
Dear Editor,
The very address, 'Dear Editor,' must have led you to instantly conclude that this is nothing but a brief from the writer to the editor for favour of accepting his article, has it not? I shall not outcaste the piece by telling you what it is straightaway. If you are willing to be patient, I shall acquaint you, by and by, with the characteristics of this object. Even though your position is not yet like that of Churchillean England — terrified of the German bomb — still to enter into something so totally unknown and unheard of before is a risk of sorts, you must concede. That is why my first request to you is to be patient, for it is only patience that pays, in a critical situation. A request only, and not a command. For if
no knowing that you'll no
TIC
TIC
TIC
TIC
TIC
Lettera
*Confessions written by Late Munin Barkotoki, circa 1940, was originally written in Assamese. This English translation is by P. Kotoky[28]

More precisely, although it touches you and me in particular, it is open to all the readers of the Āwāhan. Here there is nothing to hide. Frankly, this is neither a letter nor a brief, nor an article. On the whole, this is Something strange and peculiar. It is your privilege to decide whether to publish it or not. If you publish it, I shall be happy; if not, I shall feel hurt. But I beg of you, dear editor, please do not consign it to that all-consuming wastepaper basket of yours before looking over it from beginning to end.
The very word 'confessio
Lettera
tring
tic tic
TIC tic tic
tring

You must be rendered speechless by this extraordinary flight of my fancy, aren't you? Perhaps you suspect that it is the stimulation of some stimulant. But what stimulant? Wine, nectar, country liquor or foreign-made champagne – what? You have perhaps concluded that for me to match Shaw is like trying to catch the moon, a situation that is altogether pathetically quixotic, isn't that right? You will say that to call this absurd imagination mere illusion is to understate it – it is a story comparable to those of the *Arabian Nights*, or those of the '*open sesame*' variety. If you have a Freudian in your camp, he will invariably declare me a neurotic, or even include me in one of those all-consuming complexes of Freud. Bu
proposition is not as trivial as you
Tic tic Tic tic
Tic tic
I perspire no end, yet my thoughts do not get transformed into poetry.
tic tic
tic tic

Tic tic tic tic
tic tic
tic

ACKNOWLEDGEMENTS

In 2012, I received a call from Meenaxi Barkotoki. She wanted me read the handwritten diaries of her father, the Late Munin Barkotoki (1915–1993). She mentioned that her father was infamous for his bad handwriting and previous attempts at deciphering them didn't get far.

I went through the diaries (written between 1970 and 1993. The earlier diaries were destroyed by termites while Munin Barkotoki was still alive). Needless to say that most of the pages still remained completely illegible. Yet there was still a lot of (fragmented) information that came to light, about his thoughts, fears and impressions about life in the eighties.

The information gathered from the diaries, coupled with the significant number of books and articles written about Barkotoki, by Barkotoki himself and with testimonies from people who knew him personally, helped me form a picture of a person whom I had never met. I would like to thank Upendra Barkataki, Neel Pawan Barua and Nilmoni Phookan, who shared their valuable insights on Munin Barkotoki.

Over the next few years, this diary reading project evolved into a film project and then into a book (a biography on the Late Barkotoki) and finally into a graphic novel. For this alone I am grateful to the Munin Barkotoki Memorial Trust and Meenaxi Barkataki, for keeping faith in me, and for the steady financial support, despite these erratic shifts in goal posts.

The focus of this work was not to create fiction. The idea was to string together the fragmented pieces of information on the Late Barkotoki's life and to find an art style that I could sustain for the length of an entire book. While the storyline revolved around some of the milestones in the Late Barkotoki's life, it was Joe Sacco's *Palestine* that gave me the confidence to decide on a style of drawing and inspired me to embark on this journey. In addition to the Late Barkotoki's life story, the few incidents and characters that I had to add of my own were drawn from real life. The character of Captain D for instance is based on a friend, Dhritiman Deori. It was Deori who first told me about the missing Plutonium of Nanda Devi Peak.

Between 2012 and 2019, a few people passed away, but not without playing an important role in this project. I wish to thank them all.

Back in 2012 when Meenaxi was looking for someone to read her father's diaries, she had called the filmmaker Altaf Mazid. It was Altaf who had suggested my name to her. He passed away soon after. This project would have never taken place without him. I cannot move forward without thanking Altaf.

Some time in 2015 during a meeting with Meenaxi , I was placing my idea of turning the book into a graphic novel (we had already jumped from a film into a book a year or so ago). Also present in that meeting was Stephan. While Meenaxi needed some convincing and I had to show her a copy of *Palestine* by Joe Sacco, it was Stephan who liked the idea and mentioned a German author, Aron Schmidt. Stephan struck me as an unusual follower for 'graphic books', having dedicated his life to mathematics. Stephan passed away this year without seeing this book.

I also had the honour of meeting Renuka Devi (the Late Barkotoki's wife) and Sahitya Akademi winner Arun Sarma, who gave vivid testimonies on Barkotoki. Both passed away in 2017. I would like to believe that they would have approved this work.

The fact that this book went into print is a miracle. This has been made possible by Preeti Gill, who helped find the publisher, saving me the ordeal of having to find one myself and letting me concentrate on the book. This book is also indebted to Kartikeya – my editor for his prompt and helpful insights. The process of book writing is an invisible process. Outwardly everything appears still and as a result, it is often difficult to see a writer working. I am indebted to the people who saw some value in this book and supported me unconditionally during this journey. I am indebted to Akash, Amit, Amrapali, Ankush, Apoorva, Arif, Benjamin, Dhriti, Gyatso, Jagat, John, Kingshuk, Lubna, Nibedita, Nurul, Rajib, Ravi, Sabita, Safiqul, Sanmoni, Shruti, Simanta, Stuti and Ujjwal. I'm also indebted to my parents for providing me a home and for keeping me well fed during this journey.

Most of the work was done at home in my native village of Dudhnoi. It is here that I had found the space to work on the book in peace. For that I'd like to thank my friends and members of my community for accepting me, despite my absence from social events.

I hope this book finds acceptance among the readers despite its unusual form.

REFERENCES

1. Meenaxi Bhattacharjee, "From One Solitude To Another," in *Bibhinnojonor Dristit Munin Barkotoki*, ed. Upen Borkotoki (Guwahati: Lawyers Book Stall, 1994), 140.
2. Ibid.
3. Surjya Das, "Byotikromi Puruxh Munin Barkotoki," in *Proxongo Munin Barkotoki*, ed. Upen Borkotoki (Guwahati: Notun Oxom, 2005), 111.
4. Upen Borkotoki, "Xompadokor Prosnor Uttorot: Shrimoti Renuka Devi Barkotoki," in *Proxongo Munin Barkotoki*, (Guwahati: Notun Oxom, 2005), 118.
5. Ranjit Kr. Dev Goswami, Foreword to *A Munin Barkotoki Miscellany*, ed. Ranjit Kr. Dev Goswami (Guwahati: Book Hive, 1998), iii.
6. Quoted in Linda Anderson, "Subjectivity, representation, narrative," in *Autobiography* (New York: Routledge, 2001), 59.
7. Excerpts from the live recording of the Munin Barkotoki Award Ceremony on 2 March, 2013, Vivekananda Auditorium, Uzan Bazar, Guwahati.
8. From the speech by Dr Dilip Baruah at the Munin Barkotoki Award Ceremony, 2 March, 2013, Vivekananda Auditorium, Uzan Bazar, Guwahati.
9. Vashna Jagarnath, "The Diary as 'The Mirror of the self'," (Draft paper, WISH Seminar) https://wiser.wits.ac.za/system/files/seminar/Jagarnath2012.pdf.
10. Linda Anderson, "Subjectivity, representation, narrative," in *Autobiography* (New York: Routledge, 2001), 59.
11. *The Exorcism of Emily Rose*, directed by Scott Derrickson (Beverly Hills, CA, USA, 2005)
12. Surjya Das, "Byotikromi Puruxh Munin Barkotoki," in *Proxongo Munin Barkotoki*, ed. Upen Borkotoki (Guwahati: Notun Oxom, 2005), 111.
13. Ibid.
14. Ibid.
15. "Renowned Assamese playwright and novelist Arun Sarma dies at 85," *Hindustan Times*, 27 March, 2017, https://www.hindustantimes.com/books/renowned-assamese-playwright-and-novelist-arun-sarma-dies-at-85/story-nti8UCYvHpenKp7RwK5gIN.html.
16. "Curtain falls on thespian," *The Telegraph*, 27 March, 2017, https://www.telegraphindia.com/states/north-east/curtain-call-for-thespian/cid/1429605.

17. Arun Sarma, "Munin Barkotokir Natya Priti," in *Proxongo Munin Barkotoki*, ed. Upen Borkotoki (Guwahati: Notun Oxom, 2005), 39–41.
18. Munin Barkotoki, "Plays of Arun Sarma," in *A Munin Barkotoki Miscellany*, ed. Ranjit Kr. Dev Goswami (Guwahati: Book Hive, 1998), 32–33.
19. "The Rumpus Interview with Nanette Vonnegut," *The Rumpus*, 12 Nov, 2012, https://therumpus.net/2012/11/the-rumpus-interview-with-nanette-vonnegut/.
20. Kumud Goswami, "Obhijat Oxomiya Buddhijibi Barkotoki Sir," in *Proxongo Munin Barkotoki*, ed. Upen Borkotoki (Guwahati: Notun Oxom, 2005), 75.
21. Krishna Bhuyan, "Munin Barkotoki: A Brief Account of His Life and Work," in *A Munin Barkotoki Miscellany*, ed. Ranjit Kr. Dev Goswami (Guwahati: Book Hive, 1998), 148–162.
22. "Satyendranath Barkataki Aru Teor Byoktigoto Puthibhoral," *Amar Oxom*, 22 Dec, 2012.
23. Kailash Nath Katju, Foreword to *The Escapades of a Magistrate*, Satyen Barkataki (Calcutta: Orient Longman, 1961), ii.
24. Satyen Barkataki, *The Escapades of a Magistrate* (Calcutta: Orient Longman, 1961), 87–97.
25. Apurba Sarma, "Byoktikromdhormi 'Bismrito Byotikrom,'" in *Proxongo Munin Barkotoki*, ed. Upen Borkotoki (Guwahati: Notun Oxom, 2005), 56.
26. Nalinidhar Bhattacharjee, "Munin Barkotoki: Ejon Pranban Roxik," in *Proxongo Munin Barkotoki*, ed. Upen Borkotoki (Guwahati: Notun Oxom, 2005), 12–13.
27. Upen Borkotoki, "Munin Barkotoki: Gunomugdhar Dristire," in *Potra Sahityar Xubakh*, ed. Upendra Borkotoki, (Guwahati: Chandra Prakash, 2011), 78.
28. Upen Borkotoki, "Xompadokor Prosnor Uttorot: Shrimoti Renuka Devi Barkotoki," in *Proxongo Munin Barkotoki*, ed. Upen Borkotoki (Guwahati: Notun Oxom, 2005), 121–122.
29. Munin Barkotoki, trans. P. Kotoky, "Confessions," in *A Munin Barkotoki Miscellany*, ed. Ranjit Kr Dev Goswami (Guwahati: Book Hive, 1998), 127.